For the Love of

a Child

For the Love of a Child

Wilburta Arrowood

Publishing Designs, Inc.
Huntsville, Alabama

Publishing Designs, Inc.
P.O. Box 3241
Huntsville, Alabama 35810

Printed in the United States

Publishers Cataloging-in-Publication Data

Arrowood, Wilburta
For the Love of a Child./Wilburta Arrowood.
212 pp.; 21.59 cm.
1. Aids—Fiction. 2. Vengeance—Fiction. 3. Christian Living—Fiction.
I. Arrowood, Wilburta. II. Title.
ISBN 0-929540-35-2
813'.54—dc21

Prologue

Margaret Ceradsky stared at the shaft of sunlight which illuminated the lid of her daughter's casket. *How dare God be so cheerful on this day.*

Margaret watched the preacher's eyebrows lift and fall as he spoke. His hands fluttered back and forth, and she heard the fluctuations of his voice, but the impact of his words was lost on her. What could he possibly say to ease her agony? Had he ever lost an only child? Had he sat day after day and watched his beautiful daughter waste away? Could he even begin to guess how Margaret hated Andrew Bartimus?

Margaret blinked when she realized the preacher had paused a moment for prayer. Tears no longer flowed from her eyes, for the ducts had dried long ago. Over a year ago to be exact. She remembered the day her beautiful Angela had come home and said, "Mom, we have to talk."

Margaret tried to listen to the preacher, but she couldn't concentrate. She counted all the potted plants at the front of the room.

Margaret glanced across the chapel aisle and saw Angela's doctor sitting in a pew, eyes focused on the preacher, who continued to drone on about God's love and forgiveness.

Rage raced through Margaret. What did Angela need to be forgiven for? She was only twenty-three, and there she lay in that white, satin-lined box with pink gladioli and baby's breath draped across the lid.

A secret delight ran through her at the thought of one Andrew Bartimus burning in hell for all eternity.

Twenty-nine plants. She tried to concentrate on the preacher's words. Margaret's hands ground into one another. The whole universe seemed at peace, almost joyful, and she resented it. She swallowed the bile that rose in her throat. Dust particles danced in the sunbeam that had shifted to the floor.

The preacher said something about repentance and eternal joy.

Margaret was positive Andy would never repent, and she could, at will, call up a visual image of huge buckets of Satan's red pulsating jewels raining down on Andrew's dark head. His hair singed and smoked, and the skin on his ears blistered, broke and oozed fluid. His lips were cracked, and he lifted his hands in silent plea for a sip of water. Margaret held the sweat-covered pitcher of ice water just beyond his reach and smiled before she told him, "Burn in hell for all eternity, you fiend."

God would never forgive Andrew Bartimus, and Margaret didn't intend to even try. Somewhere out there Andrew continued to live his life and do his evil deeds, but her Angela, her once beautiful Angela, lay here in a metal box soon to be shut away from the light of day forever.

Yes, Margaret promised, *you will burn in hell, Andrew Bartimus, but first I'm going to find you and make you pay in this life for what you've done. I WILL find you, and you will wish you could die.*

Chapter One

Monday morning Margaret stood at the bay window in her kitchen and watched the rain beat curving little highways down the pane before other droplets raced along in a huge network of speedways.

The television murmured in the living room " ... clear, and sunny in the afternoon ... " Margaret smiled and remembered that her deceased husband Henry used to say, "If you don't like the weather in Kansas City, just wait a minute. It'll change." It had been a joke they'd shared often, especially in the spring, like now.

The ringing phone pulled Margaret out of her musings. She set her coffee cup on the table and picked up the receiver.

"Margaret, this is Judy at One Hour Cleaners. Late Friday evening we made a call on the Church of Christ on Glenn Hendren Drive in Liberty. They wanted some old draperies above their baptistry cleaned, but when we looked at them, I didn't think they'd take a cleaning. They're dry-rotted. Anyway, they asked if I knew a good custom drapery maker, and I thought of you. I didn't know whether you're ready to take on any new projects, but they want someone who will do the job right, and I knew you would. Are you interested?"

Margaret closed her eyes and tried to gather her wits. It had been three weeks since Angela's funeral, and she had to start working again sometime. There were medical and funeral bills stacked knee deep to a giraffe on her desk. She would have to search for Andrew in her off hours. The bills wouldn't wait, and she was certain her rage would not calm in any delay.

"Yes. Probably," she forced herself to say. "Do you know what type of fabrics they're interested in?"

Judy gave her all the information she knew, and a phone number for the preacher's secretary. "Oh, and she says he's a widower," Judy said in a teasing tone.

Great! Just what I need. A job for some lonely widower, and a friend pushing us together.

7

"I'll give the secretary a call," Margaret said. She went to the basement to retrieve her sample books and the case that held her tape measure, order pads, and other supplies. She wanted to be sure she still had everything she needed before she set an appointment.

"Hi, Fiddley," she said to the large fiddle-leafed fig next to the window. "You could use a drink from the looks of you."

She went to the bathroom and pulled a gallon of water from beneath the vanity. She poured out almost a half gallon of liquid before the pot began to drain. "I almost waited too long, didn't I, boy? I should go see about Spidy and Shiftless, too. They may have already croaked on me."

She took her work case upstairs and set it on the kitchen table before she went to the living room to water the huge schefflera in the corner. "I'm sorry, baby. You're really thirsty, aren't you? Look how you've shed, but I don't blame you for pouting. I'll do better. I promise."

She scraped up a handful of crinkly leaves and went to her bedroom to water the variegated spider plant that hung in an elaborately beaded macramé hanger. Finally, she returned to the phone in the kitchen.

Margaret hoped she wouldn't encounter an overzealous preacher. She had no interest in religion after watching Angela wither away. Margaret had gone to various churches with friends and she used to believe there was a loving God who cared for people. That was before the funeral. Now she wasn't sure there was a God. She just wanted to do this job and be left alone. If she had a choice, she would refer it to someone else. The problem was, she needed the income, and she had no other prospects right now.

She resolved to stay on a purely business level. She wasn't ready to totally deny God's existence, but neither did she feel any love for him, and he certainly couldn't love her.

Margaret placed the call to the church secretary.

"I have to leave for a while," the woman said, "but we're eager to get this project done, because we're having a big homecoming event in three months, and we'd like the drapes done before then.

Brother Forrest will be here, and he can let you in and show you what needs to be done."

"Will he be able to chose the fabrics?" Margaret asked. She didn't know anything at all about the church's protocol, but she did know most men wouldn't give a flip about color or pattern.

"If you could come today, it'd be great, because the building deacons meet tonight, and they could probably call you with a decision tomorrow."

Margaret took down directions. "I'll be there in about forty-five minutes," she said and hung up the phone.

She followed Interstate 35 north of the city to the Highway 291 exit, made a right turn, and saw the red-brick building just to the left, as the secretary had said. She couldn't see a parking lot, but a driveway led around to the back. There she saw large double-sided glass doors and a sign that read "Ring bell."

She did and waited until a man in his late forties, or early fifties, came to open the door. He wore black slacks and a light blue-and-white plaid shirt, with just a tiny bit of yellow and red in it. It looked great with his full head of salt-and-pepper hair. The tiny scar over his right eyebrow gave him a satirical pixie expression when he smiled.

A widower? Hmmm. Someone will snatch him up soon, as distinguished as he is.

"Come in," he said when he held the door open for her. "I'm Brother Micah Forrest. I'm the minister here."

Margaret was surprised at the casual attire, but then he wasn't preaching at the moment. She supposed even preachers stepped out of the limelight on occasion.

"I'm Margaret Ceradsky. I'm here to measure for new draperies."

"Oh, yes. Lacey said you would be coming by. The baptistry is at the front of the auditorium, through here." He led her across the vestibule to another pair of double-hung wooden doors.

"I'll switch on the lights."

Brother Forrest swung the doors open, and Margaret saw the moderately large auditorium in a traditional arrangement of two parallel rows of pews. A center aisle, two outer aisles, and the podium area were carpeted in plush red. The remainder of the floor was a gray-and-white-flecked utility carpet.

Margaret frowned. Reds were often difficult to match, and sure enough, when she looked at the drapes behind the podium, they were off just enough to be noticeable. She also noted how long they were.

The roof rested on huge trusses, and there was no loft. The drapes hung from the peaked ceiling in a type of valance. Below that, other straight, pleated panels hung to the top of a dark wooden wall which was a little above waist high. No wonder Judy had called her. This was not a job for an amateur, but how would she ever get up there to measure? The ceiling must be forty feet high at the peak!

Brother Forrest patted her arm. "I know. It's awfully daunting, isn't it? But we've decided to take the old drapes down for now, and you can use those for a pattern and size. Our main concern was whether you could deal with anything that long."

Margaret felt the tension ease from her shoulders. "I'm sure I can, if I'm able to use those, but I'm not too sure I want to tackle taking them down or re-hanging them. That's quite a climb."

Brother Forrest chuckled.

Margaret noticed how smile lines softened his eyes. He would put the most reticent at ease with that smile. "I don't blame you one bit. I'm terrified of heights, myself, but one of the deacons climbs up there frequently to change light bulbs, or to hang our projector screen. I'm positive he'll do whatever you need, as long as you can fit it around his work schedule."

"I'll make it a point to do so," Margaret said. "If he'll do the high stuff, I can handle the rest."

"Good! So what do you need first?"

"I suppose we can start with fabric swatches, until I can get some measurements. Do you want red again?"

"Well, that's the question. We've never been really happy with the way those mismatch the carpet, and we wondered if you could find a better shade or suggest something different. The carpet was added quite a while after the drapes were up, and the choices in red were quite limited."

"We can look. Is there somewhere for me to spread my sample books out a bit?"

"Of course. My office is just down the hall. You can use my desk." Micah motioned with his hand.

"Oh, no. I wouldn't want to intrude. Anywhere's fine."

"There's a table in there as well." He led her down the hall to a doorway on the right. When he stepped back and motioned her in, she gasped.

"How lovely! Do you grow those?" Several pots sat on shelves in front of a window, and each held a different kind of orchid.

Micah's smile broadened, so that Margaret could see how much the plants meant to him. "Yes. They're my stress relief. When things get heavy, I take a few minutes to talk to them and care for them. It helps to keep me sane."

"I talk to my plants, too, but you must be inundated with stress to manage all these."

The preacher chuckled and nodded.

"What's this one?" She pointed to a nearby pot.

Micah reached out and touched the stem full of small delicate white blooms. "It's a Dendrobium. Those on that shelf are all Cymbidiums of different colors. And this one," he caressed a huge white and purple blossom, "is a Cattleya."

"They're all orchids, aren't they?"

"Yes, they are."

"I've read they take a great deal of special care. My plants do well to get watered once in a while."

"Orchids do demand a lot of time, but as I said, they help to keep me sane. Therefore, they're worth the cost in time."

"I'm sure you're right."

Only after she surveyed all the plants on the shelves did she look about at the large desk, the shelf-lined walls full of reference books, and a copier in one corner. Along the wall opposite the desk were two easy chairs which looked comfortable enough to entice the most reluctant to relax and confide their problems. To the left was a classroom table and a couple of folding chairs.

"I know the table looks out of place, but we label bulletins for mailing, lay out printing, and do any number of other jobs, and this is close to the phone," Brother Forrest explained.

Margaret smiled. "If it works for you, it'll certainly work for me."

She spread her sample books and began to flip pages to all the red samples she could find. When she had several, she slipped them out of their plastic sleeves.

"If you like the weight and texture of any of these, we can take them in and compare them to the carpet."

Brother Forrest reached out and felt each one before he shrugged. "I'm afraid I don't know much about fabrics. The deacons in charge of the inside building maintenance will do the preliminary choosing and the elders will ultimately decide, but what would you recommend?"

"Do you think they will want to stay with the velvet, or would they like a heavy linen look or something slick?"

"I don't know. Would the linen be better?"

"Not necessarily, unless the color is better. Let's go see which matches best."

A few minutes later, Margaret chuckled. "I never figured a preacher would ever get me on my knees, but here I am on the floor."

Brother Forrest laughed with her. "Yes, you surely are." He sobered. "I take it you aren't religious?"

Margaret glanced up and saw him study her. *His eyes are brown, but they feel like steel cutting into me,* she thought.

"Not since my daughter died," she said. "I don't much like the God who took away a lovely young woman like her."

"I'm sorry," Brother Forrest said, his voice full of concern, "but have you considered the possibility that God didn't do that? Perhaps she was a victim of natural law, or God allowed Satan to exert his powers. Sometimes Satan uses people for his own purposes."

"But, as you said, God allowed him to. Believe me, I've read the book of Job, and I've considered a lot of possibilities, but I've had to limit my thinking about it to keep my sanity."

She plunked another sample against the carpet. "This looks like a good match."

Fortunately, Brother Forrest allowed her to divert him back to business.

A few minutes later, they returned to the office for her to retrieve her sample books. "I'll leave those three samples for the deacons to review. After they have decided and the old drapes are down, I'll come back to measure yardage and take the order. This sheet lists prices per yard and approximate delivery times from each mill. Since I'll have to order the fabric, I need to measure to give you an exact yardage, but just by eyeballing it, I would estimate it will take about eighty yards, and my labor will be the same as the cost of the fabric."

"Fair enough. I'll meet with the deacons and give you a call sometime tomorrow or the next day."

He led Margaret through the vestibule and held the door for her. "If you ever want to talk to someone about your daughter, I'm here." His gentle smile assured her of his sincerity.

"I appreciate it, but I'm doing okay," Margaret said. *And I'll be even better when I've tracked down Andy and made him pay. Then, maybe, I might think about talking to someone, but not before.*

Chapter Two

Margaret picked up her purse and grabbed a notebook. It would take her a good forty-five minutes to get to the Greater Kansas City Library, but she needed access to as many sources of information as possible. The local branches of the county library probably would have a minimal amount of data.

She had no idea how to go about searching for someone, but she hoped a good librarian would be able to help her find the appropriate how-to manuals. She knew Andrew's father's name and thought that would help.

She pulled her front door shut in a rush.

"Ye-o-w!" She felt sharp claws snag her hose and rip her ankle as she danced away from a hurt and angry kitten.

"Oh, you poor baby," she said when she looked down at the fuzzy orange ball which shook a front paw and whimpered a pitiful meow. Margaret viewed her ankle and saw her hose were ruined. *I don't have time for this,* she thought, but stooped and stroked the baby gently. "I'm sorry, sweetie. I didn't see you. Where do you belong?"

The kitten mewed again, then leaned into her hand and licked her fingers. "Oh, baby, are you hungry?"

Margaret lifted the kitten and carried her to the kitchen. She poured a dish of milk and set both cat and bowl on the floor.

"You had best drink fast. As soon as I change my hose, you're out of here," she warned.

When she returned, the kitten sat cleaning her whiskers, and Margaret was surprised at how tight the little belly stretched. She locked the door and set the kitten at the bottom of the steps.

As Margaret backed out of the garage, she saw the tiny cat curled in a contented ball beside the steps.

She drove out of her neighborhood onto the freeway. Angela had come this way to school everyday. Margaret felt her tears splash her knuckles on the steering wheel. She sniffed and brushed her cheek with the back of her hand. *You're on a futile mission,* she told herself. *Andrew has moved. He may already be dead.*

Maybe. Maybe not.

I'll probably never find him.

Where there's a will, there's a way.

Is it worth losing your own soul?

Do I go to hell quicker for hate and revenge than for hate alone?

Only when Andrew Bartimus has paid for his sins will I be able to address my own.

She pulled into the library lot and parked.

Inside, she asked for any books that might be helpful in searching out a missing person. The librarian started to steer her to the genealogy department.

"Oh, no. I'm looking for someone who's still alive," Margaret said.

"I see," the plump librarian in the wire-rimmed glasses and starched-lace collar said. "Some of the same information and techniques apply, but you might try the shelf over here." She led Margaret to a nearby stack. "There are several volumes, but if this isn't what you need, come and see me again."

Margaret pulled out one book, and then another. Some looked quite general in content, but after several minutes, she took three to a table to explore further.

She began to read, and she made copious notes. Time lost all meaning. Soon, however, she couldn't concentrate for the war raging inside her mind, so she closed the books, searched out her library card and went to the desk.

"Were those what you need?" the librarian asked.

"I think so. If not, I'll have you help me look for more when I bring these back."

The librarian smiled and nodded. "Happy searching."

Margaret drove through town, reluctant to get on the freeway with her mind so preoccupied as it was. She stopped at the grocery store and got a couple of cans of chicken noodle soup and one of tomato. She hadn't been hungry at all since Angela died, but her doctor insisted she had to eat. She could heat soup in a bowl in the microwave with no fuss. It eased her sense of guilt over the promise

Dr. Rhodes had extracted from her, but it was also quite easy to flush down the disposal with minimal mess.

When she pulled into her driveway, she groaned. The kitten sat beside her front door, all eyes and mouth. She stepped out of her car and heard the distraught mewing.

"I knew better than to feed you," she told the orphan. "Go home." She gave the kitten a gentle shove and hurried inside.

An hour later she sat at her kitchen table in a sweatsuit, tomato soup curling steam under her nose.

"M-e-o-w."

"Go away!"

"M-e-o-w. M-E-O-W!"

"Oh, all right. I'm coming," she said. She crossed the room on bare feet and opened the door. The kitten bolted in and attacked her big toe.

"Ouch! You little varmint. Let go! You should never bite the hand that feeds you—or the foot that could kick you. Let go!"

She pried the kitten loose and spoke softly. "Easy there." She stroked the arched neck and back.

"Easy, baby. It's going to be okay. Did somebody dump you? It made you mad, huh?"

The kitten struggled a few more moments, but as Margaret cooed and stroked, they both calmed until the kitten again licked Margaret's fingers.

"Good girl," she crooned. She again poured a dish of fresh milk and watched the tiny mite's little belly swell.

"I wish I felt like eating," she said.

The kitten looked up and blinked her huge green eyes, then shifted her attention back to the dish before her.

Margaret punched at the crackers in her bowl with the soup spoon. They sank into a mushy mess. *I wish Andrew would dissolve so easily. He's probably out on the town eating steak and having a real good time.*

"But he'll pay. I'll see to it that he pays," she muttered before she jerked the books into a better position to study.

Chapter Three

On Saturday, it was lunchtime and Margaret sat at the kitchen table, a cup of chicken noodle soup congealing into a pasty glob. The package of crackers set full, save two, and one of those lay by the cup.

The mug of cocoa had grown cold, and Margaret pushed it and the food aside so she could draw the library books and her notebook closer.

If she hadn't been researching with a purpose, she would have found the subject extremely uninteresting. As it was, she poured over the material. She had never realized how open a person's life could be if you had the right pieces of key information. Like a birth certificate, or a marriage license, or a social security number. The books made it sound rather simple to track a person if you had even one of those items, but Margaret had none of them. She continued to read, hopeful that she could learn where to get such information.

The book she studied was written to help adopted children search out their birth parents. Although she found some topics she might be able to use, she felt she needed something more specific.

She picked up a police procedural manual. Cat brushed her leg and she nudged the yellow fuzzball away from her foot. Margaret refused to give the kitten a real name, for she intended to find it a home elsewhere. Margaret had no time or interest in a pet.

"I've already fed you, and I'm busy. Go sleep in front of the register."

Cat brushed Margaret's leg again, then flopped across her foot and grew still.

Margaret sighed and scanned the index of her book, but she didn't move her foot. Again, she found chapters on birth certificates and similar documents, public records, and one on personal friends and family.

There was an idea. Margaret knew Andrew's family had moved

away, but she had no inkling about where. Andrew's father was an Army recruiter. They could have gone to any major city in the country.

But one of his friends might have kept in touch. The only problem was, Margaret didn't know who his friends were. Nor did she know how to find out. She poured over the book, searching for a clue as to where to begin.

Margaret jumped when the phone rang, and Cat sprang away from her foot when she stood.

"Mrs. Ceradsky? This is Micah Forrest. I called to let you know the deacons chose the linen fabric and the lining you recommended, and the elders have approved their choice."

The preacher's voice sounded cheerful. A warmth flushed her when she remembered his lopsided, almost boyish smile.

"Excellent. I'll call in the order on Monday. It should be here in two weeks or less."

"Will that give you enough time?"

"It should. Once I get the measurements I need, it won't take long to put things together."

"Wonderful, and by the way, I realize it is quite short notice, but I've just been thinking. You seemed to enjoy the plants in my office a great deal when you were here. There's an orchid show at Bartle Hall today, and I didn't think I would be able to go, but my schedule has suddenly cleared. I wondered if you might enjoy going along? They usually have several growers present with plants to sell, as well as to view."

Margaret looked down at her pink sweatsuit with the glitter-paint-outlined appliques. She ran her fingers through her shoulder-length brown curls and looked at her watch.

"Oh, Brother Forrest, I would love to see the orchids, but what time did you plan to go?"

"I'm Micah to my friends, and any time it's convenient for you will work. The show opened at ten this morning and will run until ten tonight. I could pick you up right away, and we could tour the hall, and go to dinner afterward. Or, I could pick you up around five or five-thirty, we could go to dinner, and then tour the hall."

Margaret gave a nervous little laugh. "I'm not sure I can go to dinner. Perhaps I should decline this time."

"Nonsense. It's Saturday, and you shouldn't be working that hard today. Besides, I had hoped you would take pity on me. You see, I eat most of my meals alone, and I search for opportunities to have someone to talk to."

Margaret looked at her watch. Two-thirty. She needed to shower and wash her hair. And she wanted to spend a bit more time on her research.

"Okay. I have a few things to finish up this afternoon, but I could probably be ready around five-thirty."

"Excellent. We'll have dinner and go smell the orchids."

Margaret frowned. "Do orchids have a fragrance?"

Micah gave a deep laugh. "We'll let you smell them yourself to see."

Margaret replaced the receiver and smiled. How nice of him to think of her. It had been years since she'd gone anywhere with a man. Not since Henry died. A warm glow filled her when she sat down at the table again.

She picked up the book she had been reading. *I wonder if he would want to take me if he knew what I was doing right now?* She smothered the thought and adjusted her wire-rimmed bifocals. *He doesn't have to know,* she decided.

She went back to her research.

"Rookies often miss the obvious resources, such as checking a telephone book for a listing for the person they're hunting." It sounded reasonable, but she knew Andy had moved. Not much help there.

At four-thirty Margaret stacked the books and her notepad together and went to shower.

Micah arrived at five-forty-five, by which time Margaret had begun to worry.

He stood at the door in gray slacks, a bright red turtleneck sweater, and a black jacket. He looked just as distinguished as before.

Margaret wondered why he wasn't married.

"I'm terribly sorry," he apologized. "I was on my way out of the house when one of the members of my congregation called and asked for the address of a former member who now lives in Texas. I had to look it up on the internet. It took a while to boot up, do my work, and turn it back off. As soon as I finished, I tried to call you, but there was no answer, so I decided to come on."

"I must have been letting Cat out, but it's not a problem. I'm in no hurry."

"Neither am I, except that I have reservations at the Savoy in half an hour, and it may rush us a bit to get there on time."

Margaret was surprised. The Savoy was one of the best restaurants in the Kansas City area.

"I hope you like seafood. Red Lobster may have more variety, but I like the individual attention at the Savoy."

"I'm not much for eel or octopus, but I love shrimp and lobster."

"Good. They do serve the latter two, and I would worry about you if you wanted the first two."

They both laughed as Margaret took the arm he held out for her. She liked this man.

"Well, I'm ready, so unless we have a problem on the bridge across the Missouri River, we should be fine."

Micah led her to his dark maroon Contour and helped her in. He drove on the freeway with experienced confidence, and Margaret relaxed in her velvet-upholstered seat.

"You mentioned a telephone directory on your computer," she said. "I didn't know there was such a thing."

"Oh, yes. It's amazing what all you can do anymore. I have internet access and can find all the residential listings in the whole United States."

"All of them?"

"All that are listed in the phone books. It's been a real help in my work."

Margaret's mind raced. "I can imagine," she said.

I wonder . . . No. Don't even think it. A preacher would never help you find someone for the reason you have. But he wouldn't have to know why I'm looking.

"Of course," Micah said, "if the person I'm looking for has an unlisted number, I have to use other resources."

"Like what?" Margaret asked, hating herself for asking, but needing his answer.

"Well, sometimes I know a mutual friend I can call, or I may have the information in the records at the church. Sometimes I know a city and can use a directory of churches. I call a local church office for the information I need. I've turned into a regular sleuth at times."

"You sound very resourceful," Margaret said, trying to decide how Micah's experiences could be used to help her in her search.

You can't use a preacher to help you get revenge.

Andrew Bartimus deserves anything I can dish out.

Vengeance is mine, saith the Lord.

He killed my daughter.

"Here we are." Micah's words jerked her out of her inner war.

"I'm sorry. We'll have to walk a bit. The parking around here is atrocious, but I think you'll find the meal worth the effort."

Margaret smiled, pushed her angry thoughts into the back corner of her mind, and determined to enjoy Micah's company for this evening.

After dinner, Micah drove the few blocks to Bartle Hall and parked in the underground garage.

When they walked into the huge auditorium, Margaret gasped. "Oh, look. Orchids everywhere!" She eyed rows of booths, each filled with blooming plants in pots, plain and fancy. People crowded down the aisles and stood gaping, talking, and buying plants on all sides.

Micah smiled and nodded. "Yes, and on the other side of the hall we'll find African violets and all their finicky relatives."

"Really?"

Micah took her arm and led her between the aisles of displays. Margaret had never seen so many varieties and colors of orchids. Each new specimen enthralled her, and the diversity ranged from tiny Vanda's to the huge Cattleya's.

When they reached a display of Cymbidiums, Micah stopped her. "These aren't too hard to grow, they're very pretty, and as you can see, they bloom prolifically."

Margaret looked at all the colors. There were lime-green blooms, and deep yellow ones, both splotched with maroon speckles, but the one she loved was a blushing cream and maroon. "They're absolutely gorgeous," she said, "but I could never keep orchids alive."

Micah chuckled. "Well, so far I've been able to do well with most of mine." He turned to the man at the table. "I'd like one of these." He pointed out a huge cream-colored Cymbidium.

"But could I pick it up later, after we've toured the show?"

"Sure thing," the man said.

Micah paid for his purchase and led Margaret toward the violet section. "These might be more your style."

Again, Margaret gasped in amazement at the range of varieties offered. "Oh, I could spend a fortune here!" she exclaimed.

"Have you raised violets before?"

"Yes, several years ago, but I got too busy to keep up with them. Now things aren't so hectic. I may just have to buy some of these, but I want to see them all first."

She browsed the tables, Micah at her side, and felt like a small child scouting out the candy counter.

Finally she said, "It's so hard to choose, but I think I like the picots and the miniature varieties, and I want to try several colors. Can we carry them and your plant, too?"

"Sure. If not, the fellow at the orchid booth will find someone with a dolly to help us."

"Good. Let's get started."

Margaret chose eight varieties in various sizes and colors, and even in the provided boxes and bags, they were cumbersome.

"This is really rather silly of me," Margaret said with a laugh. "The thing I enjoy about violets is the ease of propagation. The next thing I know, I'll be standing on the street corner trying to pawn off a plant to every passerby."

Micah laughed with her. "I didn't think about that, but maybe you need to leave the propagation alone."

"And miss out on all the fun? No way!"

They dodged their way through the crowd until they reached the orchid booth, where Micah made arrangements for some help.

After they had the plants in the car, and were on their way home, Micah asked, "Were you serious about needing homes for your baby violets?"

"I'm afraid so."

"Well, I've been thinking about that. If I provide the pots, and the soil, would you be willing to start about five dozen plants for me?"

"Five dozen?" Margaret asked in surprise.

"Well, I could do with less, but we have several shut-ins at church, and I visit three nursing homes, and if you wanted to do a few more, I often go to a group home for handicapped adults. I think they would all enjoy a violet, especially the miniatures, since they don't take up much space."

Margaret forced her smile to remain in place. Angela had worked as a counselor in a group home for the handicapped. Her college degree was in social work. Margaret knew she would like the chance to extend Angela's good intent to a group home, and of course, it would be nice to cheer the shut-ins on Micah's list.

Margaret swallowed and with great effort kept her voice near normal. "Of course, I'll start as many as you can use, but I'll mix my own soil. I use a special recipe, and it works so well, I wouldn't want to use anything else."

"I understand that perfectly," Micah said, "but I can provide the funds for the ingredients, and what kinds of pots should I get?"

Margaret shoved her grief and anger down and focused on their conversation. "That depends on what you want to hand out. I usually start off with empty margarine tubs, and I have an abundance of those, but if you want something a little nicer, we could find small clay pots at the local garage sales and paint and decorate them up a bit."

"Now, that sounds nice, but can we find enough by the time you need them?"

"I would think so, but if not, new ones aren't too expensive."

"This is exciting," Micah told her. "I can hardly wait to see the little old ladies in the nursing homes when I take those plants in, and you'll have to go along to see how appreciative they are."

"I don't know—"

"Sure you do. There's nothing that raises a body's spirits like seeing someone else enjoy the fruits of your labor. You'll have to go."

Margaret sat silent; she enjoyed Micah's company, but she knew she wouldn't be able to spend very many evenings with him. As soon as he discovered her mission, he would pull away, and that was unfortunate, for she truly liked him.

Chapter Four

A few days later, Margaret set her sewing aside and searched out Angela's high school yearbook. She studied the picture captioned "Andrew Bartimus." He had dark hair and dark eyes. She thought he didn't look like a criminal, but then she wondered what the run-of-the-mill criminal did look like. She flipped through each page searching for some clue about Andy's friends, or anyone who might know where she could find him. She had almost given up, until she searched a section of casual snapshots. One was of two boys with arms draped across one another's shoulders. She studied it, then searched the book for a name to match the likenesses on the page. She jotted down a name and wondered how to find the other boy in the photo.

On Monday, Margaret shoved Cat out the door and loaded a notepad and one of Angela's yearbooks into the car. Her first stop was at the United Missouri Bank just off Front Street.

"Could I speak with Chandler Hanks, please?" she asked the perky young receptionist at the desk.

The girl smiled. "I'll get him for you." She rose and walked into a back room.

Margaret sat in one of the modern-styled burgundy chairs and picked up a financial magazine from the chrome and glass table. She was glad the phone book had listed Chandler's number. When Margaret called, his wife had given Margaret his work number without question. She called, and when the receptionist answered, Margaret made note of the bank name, cross referenced the number in the phone book to get the correct branch, and here she was, waiting to meet Chandler. She absently thumbed through a few pages of the magazine, then looked up and studied the lobby.

Nobody paid any attention to her. She gazed at the painting on the wall opposite her seat. It was an abstract of maroons, mauves, and a sharp turquoise contrast. Much too modern for her taste. All chopped up and in disarray. *Sort of like my life,* she thought.

"Mrs. Ceradsky? I'm Chandler Hanks. What can I do for you?"

Margaret rose and shook the hand Chandler extended to her. "I'm here on a personal mission actually."

She held out Angela's yearbook and opened it to the page she had marked with a paper clip. "I've lost track of Andrew Bartimus, and I need to find him. Since you were in this picture, and you two looked rather chummy, I thought you might have stayed in touch with him."

"Old Andy, huh? I went down to Fort Leonard Wood and spent a few weekends with him after they first moved."

"Do you know his address there?"

"Well, yeah, but his dad got transferred after only a year or so."

Margaret felt the sweat on her palms. So far, Chandler hadn't asked why she wanted to know. "Do you know where they went?"

"Not for sure. There were some classified assignments coming up, and Andy wasn't supposed to know, and he couldn't have told even if he did know."

Margaret searched her memory for the kinds of information her research had suggested she could use.

"I'd like the old address, if you still have it. One of the neighbors might have stayed in touch."

"Sure. No problem," Chandler said. He reached into his billfold. "I keep meaning to clean this extra junk out of here, but I never seem to have time," he said as he sifted through a quarter-inch stack of small folded papers. "Here it is on this old list of baseball cards Andy was still looking for."

Margaret straightened. "Baseball cards?"

"Yeah. Andy and I collect. I've seen him call all over the country trying to find a certain card. He got most of them, too."

Margaret decided to make a note about the cards later, but she didn't see how that information would help her any . . . unless . . .

"Are there many collectors clubs around?"

"Yeah, but Andy pretty much steered clear of those. He said he didn't have time to spend bragging. He spent his time hunting the good ones."

"Did he have any other hobbies that you know of?"

"Nothing but baseball—and girls, of course. He loved the good-looking girls. He didn't live on base. He was in Waynesville, but we'd drive over to the base on weekends. We'd sit at the PX and watch all the officers' daughters come and go." Chandler grinned. "Yeah, he liked the girls, especially the brunettes."

Margaret felt her pencil snap, and she quickly stuffed it into her jacket pocket. She knew how well Andy "liked the brunettes." She remembered Angela's long chestnut waves before the medicine caused it to turn dull. Oh yes, she knew only too well how Andy loved the brunettes.

Margaret stopped at a Flying J truck stop, bought a map, and filled the gas tank.

"Nice day for a trip," the girl at the register said. "Going far?"

"No," Margaret said and turned to leave. She didn't intend to be rude, but neither did she choose to tell this woman what she had in mind.

She sat in the parking lot and studied the routes to Fort Leonard Wood. There were several options, but she finally decided to go through Columbia and turn south. In Waynesville she would ask the best way to the entrance to the fort.

Margaret drove down Interstate 70 through the city, using all her faculties to negotiate the heavy traffic. Once she cleared Blue Springs and the bulk of the city rush, she settled into a semi-automatic-pilot mode. She allowed her mind to wander, then romp and rage through all sorts of scenarios. She thought of Andrew Bartimus and how smug he must be with his wild past. She wondered if he had any idea how much heartache he had spread. How many other young girls had he hurt? Was he still alive?

She bolted upright. He had to be alive. She could not conceive being unable to confront him with his crime and meting out punishment for his sin.

In Columbia she turned the car south on Highway 63.

The fields were still brown from the winter kill in most places, but the wheat fields were beginning to show a slight green blush.

Margaret looked at the stark black limbs of the trees. They paralleled the empty death she felt in her heart, but they would bud and leaf again. Margaret was sure she would never "leaf out" again. She would remain dead for all eternity, for now there was nothing to live for, except to make Andy pay, but then she would truly be barren.

She found Highway 54 and followed it to Highway 17. Her mind raced with images of Andy stretched on a rack and begging her forgiveness. Then his house burned. Next his pets and his parents all died. He lost his job. His friends turned against him when they learned what a lowly piece of pond scum he really was. Those that remained fled when they were told of Andrew's vileness. None remained to nurse him as he withered into a skeletal death.

She knew some of the mental images were far-fetched, but some could become a reality, and she meant to see that it happened. Andrew would pay with all he possessed, both physical and emotional. She would see to it personally.

She stopped at a small service station in Waynesville and asked directions to the address Chandler had given her.

"That's across town, over where the best rental houses are. Lot o' people off the base live over there."

Margaret nodded and wrote detailed directions as the man told her which streets to take.

"If you get to Mable Perkin's place, you've gone too far."

Margaret shot him a dubious glance, read the directions back to him, and waited for his nod.

"Yep. You got it, and don't forget about Mable's place."

Margaret thanked the man and turned to her car. She rolled her eyes in disbelief. *As if I would know which house was Mable Perkin's,* she thought. She started the car and decided to try his instructions anyway. After all, just how lost could she get in a town the size of Waynesville?

Fortunately, she drove directly to the address on her paper. She sat and studied the houses. They were all built alike, but painted different colors. The one on the left of her designated address had a swing set, two big-wheel tricycles, and a playhouse in the yard. Margaret decided the occupants would probably be too young to know and remember Andy's family.

The house on the opposite side had faded print curtains at the windows, a porch swing with peeling dark green paint, and a bed full of huge roses to one side. A wide strip of marigolds lined both sides of the buckled cement walkway.

If Margaret was lucky, an older couple would live here. She swallowed, rubbed her hands down her black pant legs, adjusted her cream-colored bulky-knit sweater, and went to ring the bell.

After a longer-than-usual wait, she was about to turn and leave the porch when she heard the doorknob rattle. An elderly woman opened the door. She squinted at Margaret and assessed her head to toe. "Yes?"

"Hello. I'm Margaret Ceradsky, and I'm sorry to bother you, but I've driven all the way from Kansas City. I'm trying to locate the Bartimus family. I understand they used to live next door?"

"Bartimus? Oh dear, they's so many who come and go over there. It's a rental house, you know? Now let me see . . . Bartimus you said?"

"Yes. They had a teenaged son named Andrew. He went by Andy."

"Andy!" The old woman's face lit up with a glorious smile.

"Why, shore. Andy! He's the one what helped me plant most of my roses. Oh my! How could I forget Andy?"

Margaret felt her excitement grow. *Easy, girl. Don't frighten her away. Go easy.* "The roses are beautiful. I've never seen such large blooms in a garden before."

"They're all hybrids, ya know? And Andy hauled in several loads of manure from a farm out by Buckhorn."

The old woman laughed and clapped her hands together. "The roses just exploded, ya know? But ya never seen such a mess o' weeds neither. Andy spent most of the summer diggin' 'em out."

"Oh dear," Margaret sympathized. "They don't look weedy at all now."

"Nope. Like I said, Andy took care of it. He said he felt responsible since he brought all them seeds in, ya know?"

It had never occurred to Margaret that Andy would admit responsibility for any of his actions. He certainly hadn't acknowledged any responsibility toward Angela. Where was his sense of responsibility when Angela lay in the hospital dying? No, the word responsibility did not fit Margaret's concept of Andy except in a position of blame.

It took Margaret a moment to regain her composure. "As I said, I'm trying to locate the family. Did you by any chance keep in touch?"

The old woman's smile faded. "Nope. 'Fraid not. We done learned to enjoy the folks while they're there, but my hands are too gnarled and shaky for me ta write, and it costs too much ta call, ya know?"

Margaret nodded and gave the woman a weak little smile. "I see. Do you think the couple next door in the blue house might know anything?"

"No. Them and these others only been here a few months. Me and Randall is the only permanent ones in three or four blocks."

"Would there be anyone else who might have known the Bartimuses?"

The old woman seemed to think a long moment. She plucked several brown leaves off a potted begonia which sat on the wide rock porch rail. "None that I can think of. I'm rightly sorry."

Margaret apologized again for bothering her. "Oh, by the way, are there any baseball card shops in town?"

The old woman chuckled. "Mercy, child, I wouldn't know. Randall might. Hold on."

Margaret was amused at the old woman calling her "child." Goodness, she was forty-six years old. Her smile faded when her thoughts returned to her mission. Margaret had hoped for some usable clue, but it was obvious her trip had been a waste of time. Even if there was a card shop here, what could they tell her?

The old woman returned with an elderly man at her elbow. "This is Randall. He says they's two baseball card shops in town. He'll tell ya where they are."

The old man shuffled to the porch swing and eased himself

down. "Can't stand long. Arthritis all over," he explained. "You know young Andy, eh?"

"Not really," Margaret said. "My daughter dated him a few times, and I'd like to get hold of him again for a party I've planned in her honor."

It's not a lie, Margaret told herself. *It will be a party, and it will be in Angela's honor.*

"Well, Andy sure did like them cards of his. Said they'd be worth a bundle in a few years, but he liked to study the players' specs. A real nut about all that stuff."

"So I understand. Did he have any friends who liked to collect?"

"I reckon he probably did, but I didn't know none of 'em."

He gave Margaret directions to the card shop, and she headed downtown.

"I don't remember nobody named Andrew Bartimus, nor Andy, neither," the baseball card shopkeeper told her.

"He would have been the son of one of the officers at the fort," Margaret told him. "I have a picture of him in this yearbook, if you don't mind taking a look."

The shopkeeper leaned across the counter and peered at the open page Margaret held out. "Kinda dinky, ain't it. Can't see too much to tell what he looks like."

Margaret thumbed to another page. "Maybe this one will help."

"Yeah. Yeah, I remember the kid. He used to hang around with Cliff Hunter, from over at St. Robert. They spent a lot of time at the Chimney Pawn and Gun Shop, too."

Margaret felt her heart race. Now he was talking. If he could just remember where this Cliff Hunter lived, she might be able to make some progress.

The shopkeeper smiled. "All the guys they knew who collected cards liked to hunt, too, and some of their dads collected guns. Army influence, I guess."

"I suppose. Do you know where Cliff lives?" He had to know that if he knew enough to know where the boys spent their spare time.

"Naw. The local kids didn't like to be burned by the braggin' and bullyin' most of the army brats did, so they give 'em a wide berth unless they could prove theirselves worth the effort."

Margaret had to think. She had to ask the right questions, but she didn't know what those were. Somehow she had to find Cliff Hunter. He could have the key to finding Andrew.

"Did Cliff hunt much?"

"Don't think so, but the other kid did. His dad collected antique guns, too. Mostly from the Ol' West. Colts and Remingtons, I guess. I don't know nothin' 'bout guns, just baseball cards."

"Cliff must have been in here a lot for you to remember so much about him."

"Yeah. He wanted a 1957 Topps card of Hank Aaron in mint condition. He pestered me for months, but I never did pay him no mind."

"Why not?"

"I didn't figure a kid his age could come up with the money for a card that cost as much as one like that."

Margaret frowned. She had no idea what the price ranges were for baseball cards, but high school kids usually held part time jobs, and should have at least a little spending money.

"How much would one of those cards cost?"

"It depends on what kind of shape they're in, but Cliff kept saying he wanted one in mint condition. The one of Aaron on the 1957 Topps card where he's batting left-handed could run up close to two hundred and fifty bucks."

Margaret gazed in surprise. "Wow! I never dreamed a bubble gum insert would ever be worth that much. I think I'll take up chewing."

"Shucks, that ain't nothin' compared to a Topps rookie card of Aaron. It could make me a cool two thousand, if I could lay my hands on one. And a '57 Mantle rookie could get nine or ten thousand, easy!"

Margaret shook her head. "Sounds too rich for my blood. I'm surprised the kids could get that serious about it either."

"Like I said, I didn't lend too much heed to Cliff's harassing me, 'til he come in here with five hundred bucks one day and bought up some of my hard-to-find stock. I didn't have no Aaron cards in mint condition or otherwise, but after that I figured if I ever did, I'd give 'im a call."

Oh Lord, please let him have what I need. "Do you have a phone number for him?"

"Yeah, 'round here somewhere." The shopkeeper went to the cash register and clanged the drawer open. "It's gotta be right here. I don't throw nothin' away."

Margaret smiled. She could see what the man meant. Bits of paper of all colors and shapes lay scattered in the bottom of the cash drawer. She watched as each piece was examined and laid aside.

"It ain't here. I may have took it home. I do that sometimes when I have a hot lead. I thought I had a line on some Aaron cards a few weeks ago." He shrugged. "I'm sorry, but I don't guess I have it after all."

Margaret sighed. This was turning into a wasted trip. "You said he lived in St. Robert?"

"Yeah, best as I remember."

"Do you by any chance remember his father's name?"

"Shucks, no, lady. These kids that come in here have to sneak past their dads most of the time. They don't want me askin' no questions that might get 'em in trouble. Some kids spend all their allowances for cards, and their folks get a mite testy 'bout that."

"But his last name is Hunter?"

"Yep."

"Can I borrow a phone book?"

"Yeah. Just give me a second to find it."

Margaret studied the baseball cards in the huge glass case as she waited.

"Say, just what you lookin' for those kids for anyway? Did they rob a bank or somethin'?"

"No. I just owe Andy, and I'm trying to repay an old debt is all."

No need for you to know just what that debt is, she decided before she took the phone book the man offered.

She found four Hunters listed and wrote the numbers and addresses down. "Can you tell me how to get to these places?"

"Probably, but you'll come nearer gettin' there if you call and ask 'em to tell you."

Margaret nodded, handed the phone book back, and headed to the door. "Thanks for your help. Oh, by the way, let me leave my business card, and if you hear from Cliff, or Andy either one, I would appreciate a call. Just call collect, anytime."

"Collect, huh? You must owe this kid a lot."

"Yes," Margaret agreed. "An awful lot."

Chapter Five

$\mathcal{M}$argaret drove around Waynesville, just to familiarize herself with the street layout. Once she called the various Hunters, she wanted to be able to drive to their homes quickly, in case any of them should decide to make themselves unavailable.

The neat sign in front of a native-rock-covered house caused a smile: THE HOME PLACE BED AND BREAKFAST AND MERCANTILE. If she had more time, Margaret would love to explore there.

Switching on the radio in hopes of hearing the weather forecast, she turned the dial slowly until she found a strong signal.

"KJPW-102.3 on your FM dial."

A sports cast followed, then the weather forecast.

"Scattered showers and thunderstorms this evening. Stay tuned for further updates."

Great. All I need is to drive home in a rainstorm.

Margaret turned down Birch Lane, then wandered out from there. At Seventh Street, she read the sign: LIFE CARE CENTER OF WAYNESVILLE.

Thank God I didn't have to put Angela in a nursing home. I don't think I could have stood leaving her in a place like that.

Margaret remembered how hard it had been to keep her business going, but at least Angela didn't have to live in a place where strangers would strip her personal privacy away.

Margaret knew she wasn't being fair to the caregivers in the nursing homes, and she scolded herself. Those people worked hard at being kind, and she knew it, but she hadn't wanted some stranger to care for Angela.

Margaret turned the car away from the care facility. She drove to the highway and decided to check out St. Robert. That was where the baseball card shopkeeper said Cliff Hunter lived.

She took a main street to get her bearings, intending to branch out from there. She spotted a sign, Terry's Tea Room, and realized she was hungry. If she was lucky, she might find a chatty proprietor who knew the locals and could direct her to the right Hunter family.

She entered the cozy little tea room, sniffed in the lovely potpourri of aromas, and she suddenly turned ravenous. She followed the young hostess to a table near the window. Margaret was surprised at the diversity offered, because many tea rooms limited their menus to one or two special items. She expected the choices of teas and gourmet coffees, but she also found salads, croissant sandwiches, quiche, and homemade soup served in a bread bowl.

She debated several minutes before she chose the quiche. It was a heavier lunch than she normally ate, but if all went well she would be on her way home at dinner time, and she wouldn't stop to eat again.

The hostess smiled, "You'll like it. We use all farm-fresh ingredients, and the servings are generous."

"Good," Margaret said. "Do you live here in St. Robert?"

"Yes, ma'am. I've lived here all my life."

She looked about Angela's age, so Margaret thought if anyone would, this young woman should know Cliff Hunter. Margaret began to feel rather smug at how easy this was.

When she asked, the pretty blonde hostess frowned and bit her lower lip. "Are you a friend of his?"

Margaret hesitated. "No. I'm looking for someone else, and I think Cliff Hunter may be able to tell me how to reach the man I'm hunting."

The hostess sighed. "Good. I know Cliff, but he's a jerk. He leads people on and then walks all over them. If you talk to him, just be careful. He's a user."

"You mean he uses drugs?" This was getting sticky. Margaret didn't think she could approach a drug addict by herself, even to avenge Angela, and there was nobody here she trusted enough to ask for help.

"No. I don't think so, anyway. He just uses people. And he's good at making you feel real special and ripping you apart just when you get comfortable."

"He sounds like a real sweetheart." Bitterness swept through Margaret. *Just the kind of person Andrew Bartimus turned out to be. Birds of a feather.*

"Do you know how I can reach him?"

"Well, he lives on the other side of Buckhorn. I guess I could draw you a map."

"I'd appreciate that, and if you could get a phone number, it would help, too."

"I'll see what I can do."

A few minutes later the girl brought Margaret her quiche on a pretty hand-painted plate. She also served the best cup of the blackberry tea Margaret had ever tasted.

"I have Cliff's phone number here on this map," the waitress told Margaret, "but don't tell Cliff I gave it to you. As I said, he's a jerk. I don't want any kind of connection to him."

Margaret looked at the delicate pink paper with the heavy felt-tipped drawing.

"I understand," she said, although she wasn't sure she did . . . . unless . . . Oh, no. She truly hoped Cliff had not abused this young woman the way Andy had used Angela. Margaret studied the girl a moment, then gave herself a mental shake. Not every young man was as vile as Andy. Just the same, they were friends, and Margaret suspected they may have shared the same attitude toward women. She felt her teeth grind and had to make a conscious effort to relax her jaw.

She slipped the paper into her purse. "Thank you."

When she finished her meal, she drove to Buckhorn. She decided not to call the Hunter residence. She didn't want Cliff to have the opportunity to bolt, although, she realized, he should have no reason to do so.

She followed the pink map to a dirt road on the outside of town. After a few miles, she came to a farm with a large mailbox at the gate. The life-sized cutout of Uncle Sam held the box out so all could see the red letters that spelled out Hunter on the side.

Pay dirt. Margaret turned her light blue Taurus into the cedar-lined lane. The house was a turn-of-the-century, two-storied farm house with two huge black Labradors guarding the entrance and barking incessantly. Margaret wasn't sure whether she should get out or not. The dogs were big enough to tear an arm off, but both swished large tails in greeting. Maybe they just took their job of announcing arrivals a bit too seriously.

Margaret rolled her window down half way. "Hi, doggies. Are you going to let me out?"

The dogs stood facing her, legs spread in rigid stance, and continued to bark.

"Please let me out. I won't hurt anything," she promised, even though she realized she wasted her breath.

Suddenly she heard a sharp command. "Jason! Jacko! Stop that!"

Immediately the dogs ceased the noise and ran to lick the hand of the young man who emerged from a nearby shed. He walked over to Margaret's car.

"Sorry about that. They get pretty serious about keepin' people off the place. Can I help you?"

Margaret adopted her most winning smile. "I'm looking for Cliff Hunter. Would that be you?"

The man nudged one of the dogs aside. "I reckon it is."

"Good. I guess the best thing for me to do is come right to the point. I'm trying to locate Andrew Bartimus, and I understand you and he were close."

The man's mouth curved into a tiny curious smile. "Now who told you that?"

"A mutual friend. Do you know Andy?"

The man's smile widened. Margaret watched the male charisma intensify as Cliff ran his hand through his raven hair. He shifted his stance to best enhance his physique. Margaret's stomach churned. Did Andy flaunt his masculinity with such strutting and preening?

Cliff looked Native American or Latin and . . . Margaret searched for the right word . . . primitive. Yes, he looked downright primitive.

"Yeah. I knew Andy while he lived here, but I haven't heard from him in four or five years."

Disappointment snaked around her heart. She knew things had gone too easily up to now.

"Where was he the last time you knew?"

Cliff leaned against the car fender and eyed her. "Get away, Jacko." He pushed at the two dogs with his foot. "Now, ma'am, just who wants to know where ol' Andy is?"

"Oh my, where are my manners?" Margaret spoke as she rummaged in her purse to pull out a photo wallet. "I'm Margaret Ceradsky, and this is my daughter, Angela." Margaret swallowed the bitter taste in her mouth and willed her eyes to remain dry.

"Andy dated her when they graduated in Kansas City. I'm planning a surprise party, and I would like some of Angela's high school friends to be there."

Cliff took the picture and studied it. "She's quite a knockout. Ol' Andy always was lucky with the ladies, but I doubt he'd be interested in comin' to a party now."

"Why not?" Margaret blurted. It had never occurred to her that anyone would question Andy's willingness to attend a party—any party—from what she had gathered from her long conversations with Angela before her death. According to her daughter, Andy was a real party animal.

"Oh, I guess you got no way of knowin'. He got himself hitched a few years back. Turned into a real domesticated house pet, I heard." Cliff's tone turned sharp. "Anyway, he didn't have any more time for his old friends."

Margaret clucked her tongue. "That's too bad. Marriage should allow time and space for other interests, too."

"Yeah. That's what I told him, but he even quit collectin' cards." He hesitated. "Baseball cards. He had a big bunch. Worth a bundle by now, but he just seemed to lose interest."

"Where did he get married? Do you know?"

"Yeah. Out in Kansas somewhere."

Kansas was a big state.

"Do you know what town?

"Naw. Probably out around Fort Riley, since his dad was in the service, and Andy's wife went to school in Manhattan, if I remember right."

"Do you know her name?"

Cliff scratched his head and seemed to stare out past the house. "Quinella, or Quella, or some weird thing like that. I'd never heard it before."

"What about her last name?"

"Bartimus, of course." He grinned a pixie smile at her and bounced his eyebrows up and down.

What a flirt. It irritated Margaret, but she forced her voice to remain cheerful. "No maiden name?"

"Nope. Not that I know." He handed Angela's picture back.

"You don't happen to have an address?" Margaret pushed.

"I don't think so. Besides, they were movin' as soon as Quin— whatever her name was—graduated. They were goin' to Texas."

Now what was she supposed to do? Texas could be split four ways and still be larger than most states. How could she hope to find Andy in Texas?

"Can you think of anything that might help me find him?"

"Nope." Cliff leaned up onto his feet. "Seems like a heap of trouble to go to for a party."

Margaret nodded. "It is, but I have my heart set on pulling this one off. If you remember anything, or if you hear from him, please call me collect at the number on this card, and let me know."

Cliff took the paper she held out. "I'll take this, but like I said, ol' Andy cut a lot of ties when he got married."

Margaret nodded. "I'm finding he cut a few before then, too."

On the way home, Margaret maneuvered the car around a line of large trucks and pulled back into the right lane. Her mind whirled at how little she had accomplished on this trip. Four contacts knew Andy, but not one could tell her how to reach him now. Where did she go from here?

Rain splattered against the windshield until she was forced to turn on her wipers. She glanced up at the cloud bank that now raced toward her in a black churning mass.

Just like my mind, she realized.

I should let this mess go and get on with my life.

He murdered my only child.

It was not murder.

I can't call it anything else.

You're wasting your life.

It isn't worth anything as long as Angela's killer is alive.

Vengeance is mine, saith the Lord.

The wind rose so that she had to fight to keep the car on the road. Traffic thinned as people scurried to the shelter of their homes. Margaret read a mileage sign: Kansas City twenty-five miles.

The clock on the dash said eight o'clock. It would be at least nine before she could get in out of the storm. Lightening streaked the sky and the rain beat down in sheets. She flicked on the radio.

" . . . thunderstorms passing through the area quickly, with skies clearing before ten p.m."

Sighing, she pushed toward home. If only she could get her mind to clear so easily.

Chapter Six

$\mathscr{O}$nly a few days had passed since her trip to Waynesville, but with her hatred toward Andrew still burning, it seemed like an eternity. "Get out of the way, Cat. I'm busy." She scooted the yellow kitten aside and opened the door.

"Delivery for Margaret Ceradsky," the UPS man said as he held out the clipboard for her to sign. "Where do you want me to put it, lady? It's some pretty big packages."

"My fabric, I'm sure. Bring it to the back, and we'll take it in through the sliding glass doors."

The man eyed the drive and grinned. "Looks wide enough. Meet you back there in a jiff."

After he left the fabric on her cutting tables, Margaret tore open one of the bolts of deep red linen. She felt the thick slubbed texture and smiled at her mental image of the draperies in place. They would look beautiful, and this time the color would match the carpet perfectly.

When she opened a bolt of the lining, her smile faded. The ivory sateen was not what she had ordered. It would work, but she wanted an okay before she cut it.

She reached for the phone and dialed the church office.

"Micah, this is Margaret Ceradsky, and I wondered if you would be there long enough for me to run by with a fabric sample for your approval."

"I'll be here most of the day, but I have a counseling session starting in about fifteen minutes. Could you be here at twelve, instead, and I'll buy you lunch?"

Margaret was surprised at how pleasant Micah's invitation seemed to her. "I would love to have lunch with you."

She hung up the phone and got her scissors out to snip a small sample of the fabric to take with her. She looked at her watch. Nine-twenty. Time enough to bake a cherry pie to take to the preacher.

Cat sat on one of the kitchen chairs and watched Margaret work. The small yellow head cocked from one side to the other, at curious attention to Margaret's every move.

"Don't look at me like that," Margaret said. "I haven't baked in two years, and it's time I got back to it."

Cat blinked, idly licked a front paw, and stared at Margaret.

"It's just a pie, for pity's sake."

Cat cleaned her whiskers and didn't blink an eye.

Margaret turned her back and pushed the pan into the oven. "If he likes it, maybe he won't make me send the lining back," she said. "Now, you scoot out of here. I don't need a pseudo-conscience watching me." Margaret gave Cat a shove and sat on the still warm chair.

"I love cherry pie," Micah said. "How did you know?"

"I didn't, except most men seem to like fruit pies better than cream ones, and I had the cherries."

"Good for me." Micah smiled before he set the pie on his desk. "The deacon I told you about got the main drapery panels down last evening, but he was interrupted, so he'll have to come back to do the valance."

"Where are the panels? I can take those today and get started on the new ones."

"In my office. I was supposed to call you this morning, but you beat me to it."

"You were probably busier than I. Let's get those into my car before I go off and forget them."

Micah helped her carry the dusty draperies to her Taurus. He sneezed, dusted his shirt and pants, and sneezed again.

"We were going to have those cleaned—"

"It's better that you didn't. They would probably disintegrate in the cleaning solution."

"So," Micah brushed his hands, "where would you like to eat?"

"Anywhere is fine. I usually eat a fairly light lunch, so some place where I could get a salad would be fine."

"The Cracker Barrel should do quite nicely then."

It took little more than five minutes to reach the restaurant. When they were seated and had ordered, Margaret drew out her fabric sample.

"This isn't quite as heavy as I had hoped, but it should hang well. The only drawback is the R factor. It won't be quite as warm as the one I ordered."

Micah fingered the sample and smiled. "Most of the heat rises to the ceiling anyway. As high as those will hang, I don't suppose it will make that big a difference."

"I can return it or get a credit for the difference in price. It might take quite awhile to get the other one, though, because it was out of stock. I've waited as long as two months for a special order to come in."

Micah frowned. "We can't wait long enough to re-order, since the homecoming is in a little over two months."

Once the drapery issue was resolved, Margaret watched Micah pick the lettuce, onion, and pickle from his hamburger. He glanced up at her and shrugged.

"Sensitive stomach. I love them, but they make me miserable. Sort of like the brawling woman in the Bible."

"Brawling woman?"

"Umm. The writer of Proverbs says it is better to live in the corner of the housetop than with a brawling woman in a wide house. I'm better with a plain burger than with the trimmings brawling in my stomach."

Margaret covered her chuckle with her napkin, then said, "Sounds like that man knew a bit about women."

"He should have. Solomon had seven hundred wives and three hundred concubines."

Margaret laughed out loud. "Makes you wonder if he built a cover over his corner, doesn't it? He probably spent a lot of time there."

Micah chuckled, too. "It might not have been a laughing matter." He sobered. "It certainly isn't funny in this day and age. I see many families in trouble with one or both parties set on having their own way, and getting revenge if they don't. It's so sad."

Margaret swallowed her bite of salad and sat silent. The conversation was suddenly very uncomfortable. She couldn't disagree with Micah, for she could see the devastation of divorce among her own friends, but if she agreed with him . . . well, sometimes there were valid reasons for revenge. Micah might never have experienced a hurt deep enough to feel the need for revenge, but Margaret knew the agony of impotence from trying to bury a hurt. How could you be willing to forgive a wrong you would never be able to forget?

"Do you do much counseling?"

"I'm sorry to say, yes, I do."

"Sorry?"

"Oh, don't get me wrong. I love helping people. I just mourn the deep needs I encounter because so many of the problems I see should never have developed in the first place."

"How so?"

"As humans we're basically rather self-centered, and we want things to revolve around our expectations. When other people have conflicting needs or desires, we fail to use God's guidelines for resolutions, more often than not. Anytime we forget those, we get into trouble."

Micah ate another chunk of his burger.

Margaret pondered a moment, then asked, "But aren't many of today's problems unique to our times? I don't see how a two-thousand-year-old book can resolve computer age problems."

Micah shook his head. His smile lent a gentleness to his words. "The Bible says there's nothing new under the sun. You see, God created it all in the beginning and anything man has invented is merely a different configuration of something already here. In the same way, mankind is still made up with the same emotions as Adam and Eve were. Only our surroundings change.

"Man still has a need to love and be loved. He still lusts, is greedy, gets hungry, and gets hurt and angry, just as the original man did.

The first principles for dealing with those basic human emotions still apply."

"If that's true, why do so many people have such heavy problems?"

Micah shrugged, "They don't read the instruction manual, let alone follow it. We live in a fast-paced world where people function on the level of 'if all else fails, then read the directions.' That goes double when it comes to our personal lives. In fact, many people don't even realize there is an instruction manual for life."

"Oh, surely everyone knows about the Bible."

"Most do, but they view it as a holy relic or a history book, but certainly not as something to be read and applied to their lives."

"Mmm. You're probably right, but you would think they'd listen to the psychologists and psychiatrists who have evolved workable life patterns."

"Unfortunately, many do listen to all the newest trends in lifestyles and philosophies, but the only ones that truly work are those utilizing God's principles. If we would get back to those, life would be much more pleasant for everyone."

"You make it sound so simple."

"It can be, but we turn our lives into a terrible jumble when we decide to do things our way, rather than God's."

Margaret blotted her mouth. "Could be, but right now, I don't have time to discuss it any longer. I have an appointment with my cutting table, if I'm going to have your draperies ready for that homecoming in June."

Micah chuckled. "I get the hint. I've been preaching again. I must seem a real bore."

"Oh, no, but I really do need to get back to work."

Micah lifted an eyebrow, but shrugged in submission.

"Okay," Margaret said before she laughed. "So you did preach a little, but I'd guess it's an occupational hazard. I can handle it in short spurts," she teased.

Micah rose and reached for the check. "Does that mean you'll come to church Sunday and let me take you to lunch again?"

Margaret grew serious. She didn't want to grow closer to this man. He would deter her from her mission, and she couldn't allow that. He meant well, and the things he said were probably true in most circumstances, but he couldn't possibly understand her hurt, and her need to avenge the terrible thing Andrew Bartimus did to Angela. Margaret realized how incompatible their life goals were. No, she had to avoid Micah, for his sake as well as her own.

"I . . ."

"Say yes. I promise to limit my preaching to the pulpit, and you can view lunch with a lonely man as your benevolent act for the week."

"I can't imagine a man who is surrounded by so many people being lonely. How many members are there in your congregation, anyway?"

"About 175, and I love every one of them, but most of them have families of their own."

Micah paid the bill and walked Margaret to his car. "You're right. I don't spend a lot of time alone, but meals are a hard time for me. Cora and I used to sit and talk for hours over soup and a sandwich. I miss her still."

"I know. I lost my daughter a few weeks ago, and I'm still running from the loneliness. How long ago did you lose your wife?"

"Almost twelve years. I've adjusted to life without her for the most part, but meals are still hard. But what about you? I didn't realize you had suffered such a recent loss."

Margaret gripped her hands together in her lap. "Angela was ill for a long time, and I took care of her at home 'til the very last. I neglected my business, my friends, everything."

She swallowed and rushed on. "That's why I was available so quickly to work on the draperies for the church. There was a time when I had work booked six months in advance, but not now." She blinked back her tears.

Micah squeezed her elbow. "I'm so sorry for your loss, Margaret, but I'm delighted to have you working on our drapes, and I still think two lonely people should enjoy a few meals together."

Margaret watched Micah shut her door and waited for him to drive them back to the church building. Once there, she moved to her car's driver's seat before Micah spoke.

"So?"

Margaret put her key in the ignition and glanced back at him. "I'll think about it. If I'm not here Sunday, you'll have to find some other lucky lady to feed. Yours can't be such a unique congregation that there are no single or widowed women here."

Micah's laugh warmed her. "Oh, sure, we have several widowed women—mostly in their seventies or eighties, even one ninety-two-year-old, and of course, a few divorced women who are nice, but scripturally off limits for me. Besides, none of them are as interesting, nor as tolerant of my ramblings as you."

It was Margaret's turn to laugh. "So you're attracted to my ears."

Micah looked appropriately abashed. "I didn't put that well, did I? But I truly do enjoy your company, and I want to see you again."

"I'll think about it," Margaret said, "but if I'm not here Sunday, I'll be back one day next week to pick up that valance."

"Oh, yes. I'm so sorry Brother Johnson didn't have time to get them down the other evening. His baby was sick, and he left as soon as he got the main panels down."

"Do they have a boy or a girl?"

"A boy, and it's a good thing, or Ed would have developed one of the biggest tomboys in history."

"Really?"

"Yes. You see, he's a rabid sports fan."

Maybe he collects cards. He might even be useful in finding Andrew.

"Sounds like a nice guy. I'd like to meet him before this project is finished."

"He'll be here Sunday, I'm sure."

Margaret started the engine. "I'll think about it, Micah."

On the way home, she replayed her conversation with Micah. Maybe he was right about the Bible and its usefulness for most people today. Certainly, people would get along better if they didn't steal from one another—like Andrew stole Angela's well-being—or murder one another, as Andrew murdered Angela, or if they practiced the *Golden Rule*. That one said to do to others as you would have them do to you. Andrew didn't follow that one either, but Margaret would. Oh, yes. If she had committed the sins Andy had, she knew she would want someone to stop her. So she was practicing the *Golden Rule*, wasn't she? She certainly intended to stop Andrew Bartimus.

Chapter Seven

Margaret didn't go to church on Sunday morning. She couldn't see any point in it. She knew enough to know she couldn't do God's will and pursue her intent for Andy.

She spent the morning doing laundry, but between loads she watched a bit of television. It didn't take long for her to decide against that. It seemed every program was some preacher expounding some point at the top of his voice, shaking his fists or pointing fingers of guilt at his audience. Margaret didn't want to hear it. Instead, she went to the basement to sew.

On Monday she called the church office. "Good morning, Micah. I'm just checking to see if the valance has been taken down yet. I have the panels ready to cut, and I can't do anything else without that pattern."

"My, you have worked quickly, and fortunately, Ed called a bit ago. He's on his way over now. He should have what you need before noon."

"Do you think I could be of help taking down the old valance?"

"Maybe. I don't really know what all is involved."

"I could help fold it and take the hooks out of the header, probably."

"Then, come on up. I would love to see you, even if you can't help."

Margaret felt her face grow warm. Micah was nice and he seemed to like her a lot, or maybe he was just that cordial to everyone, since he was a preacher, but somehow she felt special when she talked with him.

"I'll be there in half an hour, or so."

She went to the bathroom and pulled out her make-up tray. She didn't use much: a light foundation and powder, and just a touch of blush. Sometimes she used lipstick, but as often as not, she didn't. It took less than five minutes to "put on her face."

She scowled at her long brown hair, and bunched it against her cheeks. She wondered how it would look shorter and curled into a frame for her face. Maybe she needed a cut and perm. For now she swept it up in a French twist and pushed in a couple of combs to hold it in place. She smiled at Cat sleeping on the rose-covered chair as she left the house.

In less than fifteen minutes she was at the church. Micah's car was parked alongside an older black and silver van. *Ed must already be here.*

"Come on in," Micah greeted her when she entered the building. He ushered Margaret to the front of the auditorium.

"Ed, Margaret thought she might help you," he told the man on the ladder.

Margaret peered up at the lanky young black man and gasped, "What in the world happened to your eye?"

Ed shrugged. "Just keepin' in fashion. Black and blue seem to be the colors of the season in the inner city."

Margaret ached when she looked at Ed's swollen, multi-hued right eye. "I don't understand."

Micah spoke up. "Ed's a self-appointed missionary to the street gangs in the inner city. Saturday evening he tried to break up a fight, and one of the guys vented his frustration on Ed's face."

"You're lucky he didn't use a gun, from what I hear about the kids down there."

Ed grinned. "Luck has nothin' to do with it. God takes care of me, and those guys all respect me too much to shoot me. See, I used to be one of them, 'til Micah and my wife taught me about Jesus, and I found better things to do with my time."

"It sounds awfully dangerous for you to go back, though, especially since you have that new baby."

"Maybe, but I can't quit goin' just yet. My kid brother's still down there, and I gotta get him out first."

Micah led Margaret to the other side of the ladder. "I've been trying to convince Ed that I can handle the situation, but as you can see, he has a personal stake in this."

"You? What would you be doing in the inner city?"

"Cora and I lived on Van Brunt Avenue when we first got married. Of course, it was a very nice, middle class neighborhood then. Some areas down there still are, but there are a lot of drug houses, and kids left home alone while their moms work, and most of them don't know who their daddy is. It makes for boredom—and trouble. I've tried to help that as much as I can."

"Yeah, but it's what got Cora killed," Ed said.

Margaret whirled and faced Micah. His eyes grew sad, and his shoulders slumped a bit more than usual.

"What happened?" she couldn't stop herself from asking. She knew it would probably hurt Micah to talk about it, but suddenly it seemed imperative that Margaret know. What did Ed mean, it got Cora killed?

Micah spoke in such a soft, gentle voice Margaret had to strain to hear him, even in the silent building. "We went to our old neighborhood to visit an elderly widow. When we got to her house, we didn't realize it, but someone had broken in and was in the process of robbing her at that moment. We went up on the porch to knock just as the robber burst out of the front door. He shoved me down, but Cora grabbed his coat. He turned around and shot her at short range. She died in my arms there on that porch."

"Oh, how horrible." Margaret remembered how Micah had talked about forgiveness and not seeking revenge. She had brushed off anything he said, secure in the fact that he had never suffered such a grievous wrong as she and Angela had. But he had, and suddenly she didn't understand. How could he preach and teach forgiveness in the face of such a horrible wrong. What did he know, or what did he do to be able to lay his anger and bitterness aside?

Ed climbed off the ladder and moved it over a bit. "He didn't tell you all the story."

"What do you mean?"

"Tell her who shot Cora, Micah."

"I don't think that's necessary," Micah said, sadness weighing his words.

"I think it is," Ed said. "I was the man who shot Cora to death."

Margaret sank onto the nearest pew. "What?" She felt like a phonograph record stuck on the one-word question.

"I was the man who shot Cora, and the police tracked me down and arrested me. I was tried for murder and convicted. I spent ten years in prison. But when parole time come, Micah talked to the board and got me out."

Margaret turned to Micah again. "Why would you do that?"

Micah didn't answer, but Ed continued. "He come to my jail cell every week all those years and studied with me, and he studied with my girlfriend, too. She was baptized first. Then after a lot more study, I asked Micah to forgive me, and I was baptized, too."

"You studied with the man who murdered your wife?"

"Yes."

Ed continued. "When I got out, he asked me to help work with some of the other kids in the gangs, and I did, but when I got married, he tried to kick me off the team. He says it's too dangerous."

"Well, I'm sure it is. But why would you continue?" she asked Micah.

"Because those kids are the ones who need Jesus the most. Jesus came to help the soul-sick and weary. I believe the quotation that the church isn't a mausoleum for the saints. It's a hospital for sin-sick souls."

Margaret stared at the two men and marveled. What they said didn't compute. Even if Ed had asked Micah's forgiveness, how could Micah have ever considered such a thing, let alone taught his wife's murderer about Christianity? Micah had even helped Ed gain his release from prison. Ed seemed like a nice enough guy, now, but how could Micah be sure? Why would he even want to try to trust him? How had he been able to forgive him? She simply could not understand.

Chapter Eight

Margaret gathered up the valance and hurried to load it into her car. Micah followed, trying to help her carry the unwieldy bundle. "Do you have time to grab a sandwich?"

Margaret frowned and watched him lower the trunk lid. She had not eaten, and she was a bit hungry, but she wasn't sure she was ready to spend any more time alone with Micah. As long as she believed Micah couldn't possibly understand her hurt and anger, she could justify her feelings and actions to herself, but now . . . now, she felt naked and raw. She could no longer soothe her frayed nerves with Micah's ignorance, and she resented the loss of self-justification. Micah had watched Ed shoot Cora merely because she'd been in the wrong place at the wrong time. What horrible timing for a benevolent meeting. Margaret's anger boiled within her breast.

Where was God when Cora needed him? Why didn't he protect her? Hers was a worthy mission. What more did she have to do to be protected? Obviously, it took more than a visit to an elderly widow! How could God, who was supposedly love personified, let deaths such as Angela's and Cora's happen?

Margaret jumped when Micah touched her elbow.

"It's okay, you know."

"What?"

"I said, it's okay." He hesitated, then continued. "Your face is pretty expressive when you're angry."

Margaret shrugged. "I'm sorry. I'll try to control myself better in the future."

"I'm not concerned about the expression, but the anger does give me pause."

"Why should it? It isn't directed at you."

"No, but it's eating away at you, and since I care about you, it worries me."

Margaret sighed. "I just don't understand. How could you ever begin to forgive Ed, and even if you could, why would you study with him? Why couldn't somebody else do that?"

Micah's sad smile didn't quite reach his eyes. He gripped Margaret's elbow, "Let's go into my office and talk for a few minutes."

Later, Margaret couldn't explain to herself why she allowed Micah to lead her away. He took her straight to his office and seated her in one of the easy chairs across from his desk. He walked to the bookshelves and lifted down a hinged double-picture frame. Micah's photo was on the left, and a pretty gray-haired woman's likeness was in the frame on the right. He handed them to Margaret.

She studied the photos and marveled at how alike the two people looked. They both had gray hair, short little noses, broad foreheads, and most remarkable of all, they wore almost identical smiles which accentuated a dimple on each face; Micah's on the right, and the woman's on the left.

"That's a picture of Cora. She was a remarkable woman."

"I'm sure she was," Margaret agreed, wondering how Cora would have reacted if Micah had been the one Ed shot that day.

"Yes," Micah continued. "She had enough patience to supply the whole congregation. She had to, in order to tolerate my schedule and the demands a large congregation makes on a minister, but she also taught me to be more accepting of mankind in general.

"When Ed shot her, I was so angry I wanted to kill him with my bare hands. If I could have found him, I probably would have tried. Fortunate for both of us, nobody found him for several months."

Margaret sat and stared at Micah's feet. She didn't trust herself to look at his face, or to speak, and she knew Micah would tell her whatever he felt she needed to know.

"Between the time Cora died and the police caught Ed, I struggled a lot with my feelings. I consoled myself with the passage in Luke where Jesus says we have to forgive a brother if he repents. That passage does not teach forgiveness is required if the brother does not repent. Consequently, I felt Jesus wouldn't expect me to forgive Ed, who was not a Christian, and he certainly had not asked for forgiveness, nor had he given any evidence of having repented. I hated Ed for what he did, I felt sorry for myself and the loss of my helpmate and companion, and I even found myself on the verge of hating God for allowing Cora's death and Ed's escape. Sometimes it's still hard to control all those emotions."

Margaret's head jerked up. "But you're a preacher!"

Micah nodded and sank into the chair behind his desk. His shoulders sagged, and he traced the grain of the walnut desk top with his finger. It seemed a long time before he swallowed and spoke. "In spite of popular opinion, preachers are not immune to any of the human emotions, and we are not given any special powers to deal with them. The only extra equipment we may have comes from our study of God's Word. All the while I rationalized, deep inside I knew I would have to be willing to forgive Ed. And even if he never felt any remorse, I knew I still had to get my bitterness under control. For a long time, the burden of that was extremely heavy for me."

If Margaret didn't understand before, she understood even less now. "But you seem to genuinely like Ed."

Micah's smile did reach his eyes this time. "I do like him, and I like his wife. In fact, I've grown to love them both as children of my own."

Margaret shook her head, but before she could speak, Micah continued. "Don't get me wrong. When I first saw Ed in that police station, I hated him. My hate was so strong it scared me."

Margaret knew what Micah meant. She felt the same hatred for Andrew but Micah had changed. What she didn't understand was why, or how.

"Before the police caught Ed, I read every scripture I could find on forgiveness, and I prayed every waking moment. I knew my soul was in danger if I held onto my hatred, but I couldn't let go without God's help."

"If he was going to help, why didn't he do it before Cora died? Five minutes earlier, or later, and she would have been fine. Why didn't he give you a flat tire that day?"

"You think I didn't ask those questions, and a thousand more? I blamed God for a while, but then I met Ed."

"I would think that would have reinforced your anger."

"No." Micah's words trailed into a melancholy utterance. "When I met Ed, he was incarcerated, and had been reduced to a whimpering little boy. He had spent several hours being questioned, and the policeman who interrogated him showed no mercy."

"After shooting your wife, he didn't deserve any concessions."

"I thought the same at first, but at the trial, as I listened to the defense attorney, I realized Ed had never had a chance to learn what love was, or how it worked, much less anything about God. He wasn't raised. He was literally jerked up by the hair on his head. I listened to descriptions of abuse he endured—things a grown man would have hit out against—and Ed was just a boy."

"That's no excuse for killing someone." Margaret felt the bile of her own anger in the back of her throat.

Micah swallowed, and Margaret could tell it was difficult for him to continue. "I had to have one of the elders take over my Bible classes, because I realized how ludicrous it was for me to teach when I felt the way I did."

"Surely, anyone would understand your feelings."

"Perhaps some would sympathize, but how could they understand when I didn't? I spent hours praying for myself and for Ed. I had preached about the power of prayer, but until then I didn't fully realize how impossible it is to pray earnestly for someone and maintain a significant level of hate."

Micah sat silent for such an extended period Margaret grew uneasy. She didn't believe just praying for someone would dissolve the consuming hatred, but she could see Micah did believe just that.

"So you just prayed your hatred away?" She knew her voice was sharp, but she couldn't help it. Micah studied her for a moment, and again she felt ill at ease.

"Pretty much. The more I prayed for Ed, the more concerned I grew for his salvation, and his well-being. When I became involved in teaching Ed about Jesus and God's plan for his life, I grew to care deeply about how he would respond."

"He said his girlfriend was converted first?"

"Yes. Ed now acknowledges he knew what he needed to do long before he admitted it to himself or to anyone else, but he sent me to talk to Kathy, because he didn't intend to 'get religion' unless she did."

Margaret lifted her eyebrows and shook her head. "I admire your perseverance, but I don't think I would have the same feelings."

Micah ran his hand over the leather-covered Bible on the corner of the desk. "I think you would, if you knew God and his Son as the scriptures describe them. When men like me speak about God's love and how he allowed his Son to be sacrificed for our sins, people think that's nice. It doesn't mean much until we recognize how heinous our sins are. When I realized how ugly my hatred was, I began to understand what that sacrifice meant. I quit mouthing 'forgive my sins' and started praying 'forgive my hatred and help me overcome it.' God heard those prayers and he did help me."

Margaret gazed at Micah and marveled. She knew she would never come close to understanding Micah's ability to forgive Ed, but she had to admire him for it.

Micah glanced up and asked, "What?"

Margaret opened her mouth, closed it, then started again. "I admire your strength, and I wish I could lay down the hatred I hold toward someone, but I don't think I ever could."

"Want to talk about it?"

"No—no, I don't think so. It's too new."

"That's the best time to lay it down, before it grows to you like a canker sore."

"Maybe, but I just can't."

"Would you consider coming to Bible study and starting a prayer vigil?" Margaret thought about prayers for Andy. *No way,* her mind screamed; but deep inside, she knew what Micah advocated was the preferable option. "I'll think about it," she heard herself promise.

Chapter Nine

*O*n Saturday evening, Margaret sat in front of the television and absently stroked Cat's ears. The program was some silly comedy, but there was nothing better offered, and she needed to rest a few minutes. The valance for the church was almost finished, and she would deliver it on Tuesday, but for now it could wait.

The comedy ended and Margaret went to the kitchen to put a bag of popcorn into the microwave. While it popped, she went back to her chair and clicked the remote control through all the channels, searching for something worthwhile. The second time through she paused when she saw an attractive, white-haired man speaking in the kindest, most deeply caring voice she had ever heard. She laid the remote on the end table and went back to the kitchen to get her popcorn.

When she returned, Cat rose and draped herself across Margaret's lap in a sprawl. Margaret smiled, "You're assuming an awful lot, my friend, but I suppose you can't harm much while I'm resting."

Margaret listened to the man speak and realized he was preaching. Although she held no real interest in God's word, the man's voice was so soothing and so sincere she was drawn into his message. His tone was so different from any TV evangelist she'd ever heard. He was not loud, nor demanding, but rather used a more gentle reasoning.

Margaret leaned back, ate her popcorn, gave Cat tidbits and stroked her ears as she listened.

"It is interesting that some scientists, who were formerly atheists, are now convinced of God's existence, not by necessity of creative power particularly, but by the necessity of creative design."

Margaret leaned forward. She wanted to hear what this man said about God.

"God desires, and despite man's sinful rebellion, has made salvation possible."

Margaret believed what he said could be true for many, but not for Andrew Bartimus, and not for her. She knew enough to realize God would expect her to turn her bitterness and anger loose, and she couldn't, and didn't even want to. Not until Andrew had paid for his sins.

Margaret listened as the man read the scripture: "I said therefore unto you, that ye shall die in your sins; for if ye believe not that I am he [meaning Christ], ye shall die in your sins."

Toward the end of the program the man said, "To receive salvation, each of us must first acknowledge we need it."

Margaret supposed he was right, but it didn't make sense to even listen to something like this when she still intended to find Andy and make him pay.

Still there was something about the show that appealed to her. She jotted down the name of the program: *In Search of the Lord's Way.*

Interesting title, she thought. *If someone did believe God cared, this might be a good place to learn.*

The credits said the man's name was Mack Lyon.

Cat plopped into Margaret's lap again, rolled and stretched, and curled into a contented ball on Margaret's legs. She stroked Cat's ears and sighed.

"I have to get a life," she muttered. "Saturday night and I'm sitting home with a lazy cat in my lap."

The phone rang, and Margaret reached for the receiver on the end table, careful not to disturb Cat's nap.

"Margaret, this is Micah. Are you terribly busy this evening?"

Margaret smiled and thought about just how unbusy she was, but she hesitated to leave herself too vulnerable to whatever Micah had in mind. "I'm just resting—"

"Oh, I'm sorry. I didn't mean to disturb you. I never dreamed you would be in bed at seven."

Margaret laughed. "I'm not in bed, Micah. I've just settled in front of the television."

"I hate to ask, but I have a major problem here, and I was wondering if you could help me out?"

"What do you need?" She couldn't imagine anything she could do to help Micah.

"I'm at the YMCA in downtown Kansas City getting ready for a championship basketball game, and my star player isn't here."

Margaret didn't know anything about championship games of any kind. What did he want from her?

Micah continued. "LaMont isn't here, and his phone is busy."

"I don't understand—"

"He's Ed's brother, and I've tried to call Ed to go get him, but his phone is busy, too."

"How can I help?"

"Ed lives less than a mile from you. Would you mind driving over to see if he could check on LaMont? Ed needs to get him here ASAP. The game starts in forty-five minutes."

"Of course. Give me the address."

Micah told her the house number and gave her specific directions.

"I'm on my way," she assured him.

When Margaret arrived at Ed's house, the lights were on, but it took several minutes for him to answer the door. When he did, he jiggled a screaming infant, and he looked extremely flustered.

"Hello . . . Margaret, isn't it? Come on in, and excuse the baby. He has an ear infection, and I can't get him comfortable."

"Poor little guy," Margaret said. "Let me try." She set her purse on a chair and reached out. Ed handed her the bellowing infant. She cuddled the tyke tightly in her arms, so that he could feel the warmth of her body, and she crooned softly to him.

As soon as his howls diminished to loud hiccoughs, she said, "Micah sent me. Do you know where LaMont is?"

"Yeah, he called here, and his car's broken down, but I can't leave the baby, and Kathy's taken my car to the drugstore to get a prescription. She just called. They're out of the medicine we need, so they sent her to Gladstone. By the time she gets back, it'll be too late for me to do anything."

Margaret hesitated only a moment. "Where is LaMont?"

"Thirty-seventh and Van Brunt. Why?"

"I can go get him."

"No, I don't think so. A white woman alone has no business in a neighborhood like that at night."

"Thirty-seventh is only a couple of blocks off the freeway. If you call LaMont to meet me on the corner, I wouldn't even have to get out of the car." She handed the baby back to his father.

"I don't think—"

"Don't think," Margaret interrupted. "Just call LaMont. I have to hurry." She picked up her purse and left.

She drove onto the freeway and shook her head. She must be crazy going into the inner city by herself after dark. She activated the power locks on the doors. *I'll probably be car-jacked,* she chided herself.

She exited onto Van Brunt and looked for Thirty-seventh Street. As soon as she turned the corner, she saw the boy she knew had to be LaMont. He wore a trendy Afro hairstyle, a badly worn athletic jacket, and high-topped tennis shoes.

He's a giant. Some baby brother. She pulled over and lowered the front passenger window half way.

"Hi. You Margaret?" the boy asked.

"Yes," she said before she pushed the lock release button. "Climb in. We only have a few minutes to get you downtown."

"I know, and I sure do 'preciate this. Micah says without me we ain't got no chance o' winnin'. Course he 'zaggerates a lot!"

The boy's gleaming white smile nearly filled the car. What room it didn't consume, his arms and legs did. Margaret had never seen anybody fold himself up the way this boy did in order to settle into the front seat.

He pulled the door closed and turned to grin at her again.

"You Micah's lady? I don't reckon nobody else woulda come down here by herself on a Saturday night."

Margaret glanced at LaMont. His broad grin nearly blinded her, even in the dark. "No. Actually, I'm just a friend, but I'm probably the only person he could find at home."

Anybody else would have been out having fun, or at least shopping for her family, or something besides holding a cat and staring at a stupid television.

"Good thing for me, and for Micah, too."

"Why for Micah?" Margaret asked before she wished she hadn't.

"Ole Micah needs a pretty lady around. You're stayin' to watch the game, ain't ya?"

"Oh, I don't think so. I don't want to have to get out of my car."

"I can walk ya in, and Micah can walk ya out." LaMont spread his hands wide. "No sweat!"

Margaret maneuvered the car off the freeway and headed down Oak Street.

"You can park anywhere along here," LaMont told her. "The Y's in that next block."

Margaret glanced at the digital clock on the dashboard. "We have a few minutes. Let's try a little closer. If there isn't anything near the entrance, I'll just drop you off and go on home."

LaMont's smile vanished. "Aw, com'on. You gotta stay. It's the championship game! If we win, Micah's takin' us all out to eat. He'd take you, too. I know he would." LaMont's arms flew wide again. "You brought the star. He'd kill me if I let you get away."

Margaret laughed and nodded. "Okay. We'll look for a parking spot. I can't have the star of the team killed."

She circled the block and eased into a space close to the original one LaMont had pointed out.

"Come on," he urged her. "I still gotta change."

Margaret locked the doors and literally ran to keep up with the long-legged basketball player. The sidewalk was an uphill grade, and she found herself puffing at the end of the block. She was grateful the red light held them long enough for her to catch her breath. The moment the light changed, LaMont strode off again.

Margaret pushed to keep up, but LaMont had the heavy panic door open several seconds before she stepped in.

"Micah's in the gym through those doors," LaMont said. "I gotta get to the dressing room. Thanks for the ride. Ya saved our lives." He waved his huge hand and bounded down the hall.

Margaret heard the thump of balls on the gym floor, and the noise of spectators talking and cheering. She looked up and down the empty hall, then headed toward the double doors LaMont had indicated. Just before she reached them, they swung toward her, and Micah stepped into the hall.

"Margaret! Am I glad to see you. Where's LaMont?"

"He's gone to the locker room to change."

"Good. That's good. We only have about five minutes before the game starts. The team's warming up now." He seemed to remember himself. "Do you like basketball? Come on in."

Margaret was amused at Micah's animation. She could see he liked basketball well enough for both of them.

"I don't know," she replied on the way to the bench where Micah seated her.

"You will after tonight," Micah promised. "The game's so good for these kids. We're playing the Mules from upstate. They're really good, but we're better," he said with an elfin grin.

"Who are we?" Margaret asked.

"The Hawks."

Micah excused himself and went to gather his team on the floor. LaMont raced to join them, and Margaret watched while the boys grouped, joined hands in a circle, and bowed their heads.

Were they praying? Surely not. Not over a game. They must be discussing plays. A basketball game would be the last place anyone would pray, and this group of tough guys from the hood certainly wouldn't stand still to do so.

Margaret watched the beginning of the game, while Micah paced the edge of the court right in front of her. At half time Margaret sat down and suddenly realized she had actually been on her feet screaming for the Hawks to sink the final basket of the quarter.

The score was twenty-six to twenty-eight in favor of the Mules. Margaret's temples throbbed and her arms weighed half a ton each, and the game was only half over. How in the world did those boys keep their energy up?

"So what do you think?" Micah asked when he dropped beside her for a moment.

"It's very exciting, but I'm exhausted," Margaret said. "Are the games always this close?"

"No. Sometimes they're runaways, but the close ones are the most exciting."

Margaret nodded. "This one certainly is."

"Wait here," Micah said. "I'll get you something to drink. Would you like a snack? We're going out to eat after the game," he added.

"No. A drink would be nice, but I've had dinner."

"But after the game, you have to celebrate with us. The whole team's going to Gates for barbecue."

"Man, you do know how to torture a woman. I haven't had Gates barbecue in months."

"So you'll go with us?"

"I don't know . . . I'm still by myself in the car."

"No problem. Some of the guys'll ride with you. I'll fix it."

Margaret knew she would be fine on the way to the restaurant with a carload of giants, but what about afterwards? She'd still have to drive out of the hood alone.

Micah waited a moment, then said, "LaMont told me he needs to go to Ed's tonight so they can fix LaMont's car tomorrow. He can take my car, and I'll drive yours. We'll go by Ed's house to get my car on the way to your place."

Margaret shrugged, "You seem to have it all under control. How can I refuse such a well-thought-out plan?"

Micah flashed her a triumphant grin. "You can't," he said before he patted her knee and rushed back to the floor.

"I'll be back right after the game," he said over his shoulder, before he joined the team at courtside.

Margaret watched the boys join hands again. *They must be planning strategy. That cannot be prayer.* The group broke apart and went onto the court to begin the final half of the game.

At the end the score was ninety-six to ninety, Hawks' game, and the gym exploded into jumping, shouting, jubilant spectators. Margaret pulled her head down between her shoulders and cupped her hands over her ears when the boys on either side of her put their fingers in their mouths and let out simultaneous whistles. She laughed and bounced along with them when their girlfriends grabbed her hands, jumped up and down, and screamed.

Margaret was thankful when Micah finally broke away from the group and came to guide her outside to her car. By that time, most of the crowd had dispersed, and it was much quieter. On the street, a few couples still rushed to nearby cars, but most were already gone.

"LaMont said he would ride with you over to Gates, and I think Hector and Yin Ling will, too. That should be enough to keep you safe from here to there."

"I should think so—if they all get along."

Micah nodded. "I know. I'm rather proud of that little trio. Not many of the hood kids can cross the racial lines, but basketball and prayer do seem to work wonders down here."

Margaret blurted, "So you were praying in there?"

"Of course. How else could we keep such a group together, and how could they possibly win a championship without God's help? Every last one of those kids has been told repeatedly what losers they are, and how they always will be losers. Not a winner in the bunch— 'til this basketball season." Micah grinned and laid his arm around Margaret's shoulders. "It just makes you want to hug someone."

Later, on the way home, Margaret marveled again at Micah's ability to forgive, and to become involved with the very element of society—and specifically, the same persons—who killed his wife. Margaret saw for herself this evening how much Micah cared for the team, and his enthusiasm was contagious. She had enjoyed herself more than she had in years, but how had Micah been able to overcome his anger and work with these kids and keep his sanity?

It was a puzzle she had no idea how to solve, but somehow, it was beginning to seem important to learn.

Chapter Ten

Margaret moaned when she heard Cat's insistent mew, and winced when she felt the kitten land on the bed and walk the length of her.

"It's Sunday morning. Go away," she told her persistent pet.

Cat mewed again, and Margaret opened one eye. Cat looked at Margaret and cried again. "Meow . . . MEOW!"

Margaret muttered about how lonely Cat would be without a home, but then she threw back the coverlet and slipped on her robe. She glanced at the clock. Seven.

She went to the kitchen and started the coffee, shoved a toaster pastry into the toaster, and stepped outside to get the newspaper. She smiled at the thought of last night's game. Micah was such a nice man, and he'd taught those kids a few things about manners, too.

She sat at the table and scanned the paper while she munched her breakfast. Cat brushed Margaret's leg and gave an insistent mew.

She absently sprinkled a few morsels of cat-chow in Cat's bowl, then returned to the paper and flipped to the sports section. On page six she saw the article she sought: "Hawks Vie for Championship." She read the entire piece, then set down her coffee cup.

The writer spoke of scholarships made available to members of both championship teams. A local businessman made the offer to each player as long as he agreed to stay drug free, did not associate himself with a known gang, and maintained a B grade average or better. Micah had truly done some heavy-duty work to get that accomplished.

Margaret smiled and gulped down the remainder of her coffee. "Get out from under my feet, Cat! I'm going to church this morning."

Margaret felt ill at ease as she approached the church building. She saw families scurry from the parking lot to the glass doors. She could see the vestibule full of people between her and the auditorium. She swallowed and decided she would just ease past them and sit near the back.

She walked in and focused on the double-hung doors across from the entryway. Before she had taken more than a few steps someone grasped her arm.

"Hello, Margaret. It's good to see you here." She turned toward the deep voice and the woodsy aroma. Ed held out his hand in greeting.

Margaret smiled and felt her tension ease a bit. "Hello, Ed. How's the baby this morning?"

"His fever broke, but he didn't sleep much until after three."

"Poor baby. And you're here after being up all night?"

"Yeah. I thought Kathy might be able to sleep while he does this morning, and I'll stay with him while she comes to worship tonight. Come on in. I'll introduce you to some of the others."

Ed led Margaret to a pew about a third of the way from the back. "We have class back here, then move up toward the front for worship," he explained.

They were barely seated when a man took his place at the lectern.

The lesson was on I Corinthians, chapter thirteen, and the teacher said it was often called the love chapter of the Bible. Margaret spent most of the hour trying to reconcile, to Micah's life and her own, the things being taught. Somehow, it didn't seem to all fit together the way these people said it should.

When class ended, Ed urged Margaret to a spot closer to the front. "Have you been to one of our services before?"

"No. This is my first."

"Maybe I should explain a little about what will happen."

Margaret hadn't been to a real worship service in years. Her grandmother had taken her to church when she was quite young, but then she and her parents had moved to a town over a hundred miles away. Margaret's parents were too busy making a living, so Margaret forgot about church. There was always something else to do on Sunday. During all that time she'd believed in God, but now that He'd let Angela die, Margaret wasn't really sure what she believed, except she knew if God was real, she was very angry at him. That preacher on TV said some unbelieving scientists had changed their minds and now believed in God, but as far as she was concerned, the jury was still out over whether he still cared about people today.

She pushed her anger down and smiled at Ed. "I appreciate your concern. I am sort of lost."

"Not as much as Kathy and I were."

Margaret looked at Ed in awe. She hadn't thought about how intimidating a worship service would have been to someone with Ed's background. The thought gave her a deeper respect for this young man.

Ed explained the order of the service, and she glanced around at the people moving into the pews around her. She sensed someone had stopped beside her, and she turned to see who it was.

"Good morning, Margaret," Micah said. He extended his hand and clasped hers in greeting a bit longer than was strictly necessary. "We're so pleased you decided to join us this morning. You picked a beautiful day to come."

"Yes, I did, but then I've heard you preachers think every day is beautiful."

"I see my reputation precedes me," Micah joked in response. "But I am thankful you're here and—"

"And?"

"And, I would love to have company for lunch?" His eyebrows lifted in question.

When Margaret hesitated, he rushed on. "It could be called a benevolent act on your part, because I'm sure I'll preach a better sermon if I have your company to look forward to afterward."

Margaret playfully scolded: "Shame on you. You should be focused on your lesson."

"Okay, so I stretched it a bit. But I would be happier. Won't you please say yes?"

Ed stepped in. "It may be the only decent meal he eats all week."

"Really?" Margaret didn't even try to hide the surprise in her voice.

"Yeah, he calls stuff like canned soup, yogurt, or a granola bar food."

Margaret shrugged. "Sounds rather familiar, actually."

"Then you both need a decent meal. Say yes!"

Lunch was leisurely, and over dessert Margaret felt more relaxed than she had in months. She and Micah talked about various people Ed had introduced to Margaret. She gazed at Micah, but her mind whirled. How could these people be so trusting and so forgiving?

Micah waited in silence until Margaret grew uneasy. Finally she swallowed and spoke. "Micah, do you really believe God will forgive Ed for his murder?"

Micah nodded. "Yes, I do. He already has. He promises to forgive all our sins if we will turn from them and seek forgiveness through Christ. When we follow God's pattern for living, he promises all his blessings in abundance. God has never broken a promise."

Her next question was little more than a whisper. "Do you think he could forgive someone who is consumed with hate?"

"Yes and no."

Margaret stared at Micah. His furrowed brow told her he was serious. "What do you mean?"

"God has not promised to forgive an unrepentant sinner, but if that person is truly sorry, asks for forgiveness and resolves to quit hating, and replaces hatred with love, then, yes, God will forgive him. God does not promise to forgive those who do not repent and ask for forgiveness. Neither does he expect us to forgive others if they don't ask."

Margaret pulled herself up taller. "I don't understand. I thought you believed you have to forgive anyone of whatever wrong they have done. That's what you did with Ed."

"Yes, but only after he asked my forgiveness. If you really study the scriptures, you will find we are required to be willing, and for our own well-being we need to put away the bitterness, but God's forgiveness, per se, is only available to those who ask. I don't believe he requires more of us than he gives himself."

"How do you put away the bitterness without forgiving?"

"You turn it over to God to handle. When we accept that God is just and all-knowing, we realize he can handle it, and we don't have to. We just have to step back and let him. Again, we have to be willing to forgive, if the person asks, but God is the one who judges. In his infinite wisdom, he will judge and either forgive or condemn."

"I'm not sure I can do that," Margaret all but moaned.

Micah spoke softly. "Want to tell me about it?"

Margaret hesitated, but finally nodded. "Yes, I think I do, but not here. Let's go to my house for coffee."

"Good idea." Micah rose and led her to the car.

Margaret sat at the kitchen table and gripped the coffee mug with both hands. Her knuckles glowed white against the red fingers.

"There's a man who is directly responsible for my daughter's death. I hate him. It eats at me day and night to think of Angela dead, and that irresponsible . . . man has gone free." Her voice faltered. "I've tried to find him. I want to ruin his life the way he's destroyed mine."

Micah nodded. "I felt those same emotions after Cora's death. Her death seemed such a waste, and it was so unfair for her killer to go free."

"How did you get past it all?"

"A lot of prayer, and a good friend to listen to me."

"Most of my friends disappeared before Angela died."

Micah reached over and patted her hand. "I'm available any time, day or night, Margaret, and I can help you pray, too."

Margaret traced a flower in the tablecloth with her fingernail. "I'm not sure I'm ready to turn this loose. I'm still too angry."

"Give it some time, Margaret, but let's start to pray about it now."

Margaret looked up through tears that welled in her eyes and nodded.

Micah took her hands, bowed, and spoke.

> "Father, we come glorifying your name, for we know you are all powerful, and only through you do we have our being, and all the blessings we enjoy. Father, you alone know how deep Margaret's anger runs, and only you, and your love, will be able to dis-

lodge it and replace it with good things. We ask you to start working your healing on her heart, and let her receive your blessing of peace. Help her to study your word, so that she may come to know you and your love for her. We ask through your Son's name, Amen."

Micah moved closer and hugged Margaret, and she felt herself lean into his embrace. His arms felt so comforting—so right.

Micah squeezed her hand. "You're headed in the right direction. Now, all you have to do is keep the momentum going. You are a special lady, and you're becoming very important to me. I'll help you find your way."

Margaret wasn't sure anyone could help her. She wasn't even sure she wanted any help. She needed to hold onto her anger. Her goal was to make Andy sorry for his transgressions. She couldn't do that and do what Micah advocated, too. She realized the anger made her bitter, and she didn't like that characteristic, but she could work on it after Andy had paid his debt of guilt. To just lay that down was more than she could bear to contemplate. She definitely needed more time.

Margaret gazed at Micah through watery eyes, and she swallowed the lump in her throat. Her eyes closed and she coveted the first feelings of being cherished she had experienced since Henry died ten years earlier. She worried about not being able to meet Micah's expectations, but she'd been honest with him, so he knew how she felt. Even now he cared for her, and she had begun to care for him. Long ago, she had decided she would never have these womanly feelings again, but she had been wrong . . . so very wrong.

For the next several nights Margaret slept fitfully. She began to shut Cat up in the kitchen, because the stupid creature kept trying to sleep on the foot of Margaret's bed. She had never slept with an animal, and she didn't intend to start now. Cat could yowl all night if she wanted to, and it wouldn't make one whit of difference . . . except it did.

Margaret awoke repeatedly to Cat's mournful me-o-w. Well, she could get used to that wicker bed with those old towels. She was just a cat, not the ruler of the house!

The next Saturday evening Margaret watched the clock and made sure she had her bowl of popcorn ready before Mack Lyon's TV show came on. Margaret enjoyed the hymn at the opening of the program, but her real interest lay in the sermon. Again she was impressed with the speaker's calm, gentle delivery. He reasoned with his audience, but he didn't try to pound points into their brains.

Margaret soaked in the full program while Mr. Lyon spoke about man and his salvation. He explained how simply accepting Jesus into your life, or going to the altar and praying, or even repeating the sinner's prayer were not enough, according to the Bible.

Margaret didn't agree. Why wouldn't any one of those things be sufficient? If a person's heart was right, wouldn't God accept that? The man might be kind, but he couldn't be right about this. She knew too many good people who had done those things and they said they had a relationship with God.

Still, she listened, and Mr. Lyon went on to quote what he called the *Great Commission* in Matthew 28:18-20, Mark 16:15-16, and Luke 24:44-51. Margaret wrote those down and decided to read them again later.

It disturbed her even more, though, when he told of Peter's first sermon on the day of Pentecost when he told the whole audience to repent and be baptized. She jotted down Acts 2 and decided she needed to read it also.

Though she questioned some of Mr. Lyon's conclusions she couldn't help admiring his confidence when he closed by saying, "My friend, I am comfortable with telling you what the Bible says, and I pray you will receive it and do it."

She'd never heard a preacher state such confidence so calmly and gently. She knew she needed to sit down with her Bible. She also knew it would hold the answers she needed.

Several mornings later, Margaret swallowed a quick cup of coffee and hurried down a piece of dry toast, sprinkled some kitten chow in Cat's bowl, and rushed to the basement to continue work on the draperies.

She ran her hand across the slubbed surface of the linen and felt a pang of remorse. How like life this piece of fabric was: smooth for the most part, but with little bumps scattered throughout, and once in a while a big bump. In the fabric, those slubs blended to make an interesting and beautiful whole.

Margaret reflected on the bumps in people's lives: lost jobs, moving away from friends, illnesses, divorces, and deaths. Margaret grew angry. How could the God Micah talked about allow those terrible things to happen? If he was so loving, why did innocent people get hurt so deeply?

She jerked her thoughts away from that troubling area and concentrated on measuring the drapery panels into the correct dimensions.

She worked all morning and grew irritated when Cat came downstairs and twined herself around Margaret's legs.

"Get out of the way, you pesky creature. I can still send you packing."

Cat rubbed against Margaret's leg, blinked, and mewed. Margaret nudged her away. "Scoot."

Margaret leaned over the cutting table but felt Cat brush against her other leg.

"Mew . . . Mew . . . Mew." Cat's cries were soft, but insistent.

Margaret glanced at her watch. Noon. "Now I've done it," she muttered. "I give you a few tastes of my tuna sandwich, and suddenly you can tell time!" She went back to her cutting.

Cat mewed again and rubbed herself between Margaret's ankles.

"Oh, all right. I'm coming. But it's soup today. You don't get any," she warned.

At the top of the stairs, Margaret turned to the front door and checked the mailbox. It was stuffed with the usual junk, but there were a few pieces that looked important. Gas bill, water bill, magazine give-away. Nobody here would ever win one of those. Oak Park High School? Now, what could that be?

Margaret turned the envelope over. It was addressed to Angela. It had been almost five years since Angela graduated from there. What could they want now?

Margaret walked to the kitchen and tossed the other mail on the table. She tore the letter open.

Dear Classmate,

You are invited to our five-year class reuion . . .

Margaret quickly scanned the page and flipped it up to the second, which was a form to be filled out and returned.

A class reunion. Margaret didn't realize she was crying until she felt tears splash her hands. She rubbed them on the leg of her slacks. Angela missed the two-year reunion because she had worked two full-time jobs all summer, saving money to go back to college to get her degree. She had been torn between the reunion and missing work that night. In the end, she couldn't leave the group home for developmentally disabled understaffed for the night. Those people needed her and she would not let them down, but she promised herself, and her mother, that she would go to the five-year reunion, no matter what.

Margaret glanced at the row of juice glasses on the window ledge. Each was covered in foil, a violet leaf poked through a hole to extend into the water below. Each one had tiny, hairy roots beginning to form. Soon they would be ready to pot, and she would send some of these new plants to the group home where Angela had worked.

Margaret grabbed one of the pink tissues from the counter and blew her nose. Some day she had to quit crying, she told herself.

She got out a pan, opened a can of soup, and set it to heat.

So many things Angela missed. Oh God, why? Why would Angela never attend a reunion? Why would she never be able to utilize her degree in social work? Why would she never marry and bear the grandchildren Margaret longed to hold? Why? Margaret's mind screamed.

She threw the letter on the table and rushed to pull the bubbling soup off the burner just before it boiled over. She poured it into a bowl and filled the pan with water to soak in the sink. She blew her nose again, then rinsed her hands.

She tilted the chair to dump Cat onto the floor. "Scat! I'm telling you, you're irritating me. Now, get, before I take the spray bottle after you."

She looked at the soup, sighed, and sat down. Her appetite had flown, but she knew she needed to eat. She thumbed through the stack of mail and laid it aside, except for the reunion letter.

There was to be a dinner in July, along with various get-re-acquainted activities.

At the bottom of the letter were the names of several class members whom nobody knew how to locate.

The letter recipients were asked to contact Susan Heffler, and there was even an address and phone number, if anyone knew where any of those people were.

Margaret straightened in her chair and scanned the list. Andrew Bartimus' name was not there. *Susan Heffler must know where he is.*

Margaret reached for the phone.

Chapter Eleven

Margaret didn't even have to offer an explanation for wanting Andy's address. Susan was congeniality itself.

"The address we have is in Texas. Let me see . . . here it is. Corinth. It's on Fairview Drive. I'm assuming Andy's still there. At least we haven't gotten the letter back, but I heard he was having a lot of personal problems."

"Really?" Margaret asked, hugging close a sense of "maybe there is some justice left in the world after all."

"Yes. Someone told me he got married and had a couple of kids."

"A family does seem to drag some men down," Margaret agreed, the anger at Andy having children to love and hold almost suffocating her as she gripped the phone.

"Oh, I didn't mean that. I don't have any idea how he felt about the responsibility. I think he has a real promising business."

"What does he do?"

"Computer science, I think. He sets up business networks or something like that. You know, a bunch of technical stuff."

"He should do rather well with that, I would think."

"Yes, but I heard the kids were twins, and his wife died giving birth. I feel so sorry for Andy. I mean, I can't imagine any man trying to raise two babies by himself."

Margaret felt herself gritting her teeth. Her dentist had warned her she was damaging them under all the stress. He even suggested a bite splint. If she didn't accomplish her mission soon, she knew she would have to give in; but now success looked more promising than ever. Andy was in Texas.

"Thank you for your help," Margaret told Susan and hung up.

She remembered Micah's computer directory and decided to try the telephone directory assistance to verify Andy's address.

After several minutes, the long-distance operator told her, "I'm sorry. I don't have a listing for an Andrew Bartimus in Corinth, or any of the other suburbs of Dallas."

"Thank you." Margaret replaced the receiver and sank onto the kitchen chair.

Andy's in Texas. I know he is, but why isn't he listed in the phone book? I should have asked about computer consultants. There's probably a hundred in a town that size. If he lived there and the number was merely unlisted there would have been that stupid recording about it being unpublished.

The phone rang and startled her out of her deep thoughts.

She didn't know how long she had sat there, but Cat lay curled in sleep on her lap. She stood and dumped the hapless kitten again.

"Margaret, it's Micah. I called to see if I could interest you in dinner, and I would like to take you to church, too. Could I pick you up Sunday morning?"

Margaret smiled. If subtlety was the work of the devil, Micah certainly didn't need to worry. "Dinner sounds nice, but I think I'll be out of town Sunday."

"Going some place interesting?"

"I hope so. I think I'll spend the weekend in Texas. It should be a little warmer than here, and I need a break."

"Sounds warmer, but are you ready for life on the ranch?"

"What?"

"The ranch. You know, Texas is all ranch and cactus."

"Oh, I don't think so. I'll be in Dallas. That's a pretty modern city from what I hear. Of course, I could be wrong." Margaret laughed out loud.

"Okay, so I watch too much television, and I think in stereotypes; but I have a good heart, and I like to eat. If you won't come to church, will you at least have dinner with me?"

Margaret forgot her resolve to avoid Micah. "I would be delighted, if you make it some place simple."

"It doesn't come much simpler than The Smokehouse in Gladstone. Do you like barbecue?"

"It's one of my favorites. There used to be days when I would almost kill for a barbecue pork sandwich."

"I can relate to that. I'll pick you up at six, if that's okay."

"I'll be ready."

Margaret poured the soup in the disposal, rinsed the pan and her bowl, and thumbed through the phone book to call for plane reservations to Dallas/Ft. Worth.

Micah picked her up promptly at six, and they drove straight to The Smokehouse. Micah was unusually quiet, and Margaret hesitated to break the silence. He seemed to be wrestling with some terrible opponent, and she feared a distraction might make him lose the battle.

She watched the brown pastureland in this small undeveloped area along Highway 152 and marveled that the city sprang up all around them, yet this one patch of earth lay untouched by the land-greedy developers. She wondered how long it would remain clean and beautiful.

Micah stopped at the traffic light at North Prospect and turned to her. "I'm sorry. I haven't intentionally ignored you. I just left a counseling session, and it's still haunting me. I promise I'll try to lay it down."

"I don't mind. Sometimes I get caught up in turmoils and forget all about who I'm with and what I'm doing. I think that's perfectly natural when you care about an issue deeply." Margaret continued, "Is this something I can help with? Since I don't know any of the people in your congregation, I can't exactly be a threat to anyone by knowing whatever you need to talk about."

"I appreciate the offer, but I don't think talking about it will help. I just have to decide which direction to go with my advice. I try not to make too many direct suggestions but let people discover the things they need to know on their own, with a minimum of guidance from me. They seem to take possession of the information better if they earn it rather than someone giving it to them."

"I hadn't thought about that, but I'm sure you're probably right. The next question is, how in the world do you arrange that?"

"Exactly. There are times when it isn't too hard, but this time I'm really struggling. There's a family that has suffered a great wrong from someone, and each one is bent on revenge. It's such a self-destructive mission, I want to help them all. But if I address the older family members, I am afraid I'll alienate the children, and if I address the children, the parents will feel the solution is juvenile and has no importance for them."

Margaret squirmed. "Is revenge the only topic you address in your counseling?" she snapped before she realized how sharp her tone was.

Micah glanced at her, his eyes flared in surprise. "No, of course not. It just happens this is a family I'm seeing rather frequently, and that's their major hurdle. If I can get them over this, the other issues will be minor in comparison; or at least, I hope they will be."

Margaret bit her lower lip and murmured, "I didn't mean to sound so snappy. I just wondered why someone would make a big production out of some everyday issue. If it was murder, I would say go for it; but not many of us have to deal with a murder in our lives." She tasted the bile in her mouth and felt the familiar burning in her stomach.

Micah nodded his head. "You're right. Not many of us do, but even those of us who have must be willing to forgive, if we expect God to forgive us when we stand before him."

Margaret shot a glance at him. He had said "even those of us who have." How could he be so calm after he had suffered his loss to a murderer. It was too ridiculous to even contemplate. Cool, calm, gentle Micah, who raised orchids and preached forgiveness. He knew the true hurt from that violent kind of loss. It was easy enough to spout platitudes when you hadn't suffered the wrongs. It was something else again when you had. What was his secret?

"What terrible thing happened to this family?"

"I'm sorry, I'm not at liberty to say, but it was enough for them to be angry for many years. Even now the wound is as fresh as that first day, because they take it out and rub the skin off it frequently."

"Maybe there's a reason for that."

"In their view, there is, but what they don't see is the damage it's doing to their lives. They can't drive across town, because they might run into the other family. They can't go to a movie, because one of the children might be there. They drive to one of the other suburbs to buy their groceries to keep from running into any of the offensive family. They've altered their entire lifestyles to accommodate their hate."

Margaret reflected on her own life. Her lifestyle changed when Angela grew ill. It changed even more when she died. Now it was changed yet more. Margaret had never traveled alone—until Angela died, that is. Now she would go wherever necessary to find Andrew Bartimus and make him pay for his sin.

"I just wish I could get this family refocused on Jesus and the Word, rather than revenge. Their lives would be so much happier, and their souls in a much safer position."

"Maybe so, but there can be a certain satisfaction in revenge served up appropriately, too."

"No, I don't think so. Whatever they could plan as an equalizer would never come off quite equal, and there would be retaliation from the other side, and on it would go. There's an adage that you can't get ahead by getting even, and that's true. I want these people to get ahead, and find forgiveness and peace in following the New Testament standard for living."

"Love your neighbors?"

"Um-hum. Love defuses every potential explosion if we just use it. Unfortunately, not many of us remember to use its power when we're as angry as this family is."

Margaret listened, but deep inside she knew if she agreed with Micah, she would have to cancel her trip to Dallas. She would have to face her position in God's sight. Even if what Micah said were true about God not forgiving until the sinner asked, it didn't change anything for Margaret. She knew Andrew would never ask, so she would never have to forgive. The bitterness part bothered her, but she'd deal with that later. If she let it go, she would have to love a murderer, and she was not ready to do that. Not now. Not ever. Not until Andrew Bartimus had paid his debt in full.

Chapter Twelve

*O*n Friday morning, Margaret set out extra cat chow and water, and headed to the airport. Her heart raced. If all went well, she would soon know exactly where Andrew lived. What would she do, and what would she say to him when they finally faced one another?

She knew what she wanted to do. She wanted to squeeze her fingers around Andy's throat and watch his eyes bulge from their sockets. She wanted to see him grow limp, just as Angela had done in Margaret's arms. But she knew she would never be able to do it. Even if she had the physical strength to overpower Andy, she would have to stop short of killing him. She knew that as well as she knew her anger, but then death was too easy. She wanted Andy to suffer, and he would. She would see that he did. She could make him face his guilt in Angela's death. She intended to expose his sins to himself, and to the world.

She could make sure his employees and his neighbors knew what he was. The whole world would know—and if he moved, she would follow him. Everywhere Andy descended Margaret would spread enlightenment. Margaret intended to insure his suffering for the rest of his life, just as Angela had suffered.

At Dallas/Fort Worth Margaret bought a city map, then rented a car and headed to Corinth. She stopped at a McDonald's and ate while she plotted her course to Fairview Drive.

Her stomach lurched from nervousness, and she dug in her purse for an antacid. She pored over the paper while she crunched the cherry-flavored tablets. She refolded the map and hurried back to the car.

Traffic was heavy, but it didn't take long for her to reach the correct exit. She studied the street signs and stole quick glances at the map.

Fairview Drive. There it was! Margaret turned onto the street and took in the row of two-story houses with wood siding and brick veneer fronts. *Nice neighborhood.*

As she drove slowly down the street, she saw a few one-story, ranch-style homes, and she searched each building for the appropriate number.

Her hand slipped on the steering wheel, and she realized her palms were sweating. She rubbed one hand, then the other, on her slacks. *In a few minutes, I could be facing Andrew Bartimus.*

Margaret swallowed the lump in her throat and parked. Then she checked her written notes to be absolutely sure this was the address Susan Heffler had given her. It was.

She frowned. A real estate sign stood in the yard, and the grass needed to be cut. The doors and windows were all closed; draperies were drawn across the windows. It was warm enough to open up a house, but not blistering hot yet, as Margaret knew it would be later in the summer. Maybe Andy had to work today.

He can't be gone. I've come so far, and I have to see him.

Margaret stepped out of the car and strode toward the doorway. Her shoes made military sharp clicks on the sidewalk, and she pulled herself as erect as possible.

When she pushed the button, she could hear the bong, bong, bong of a chime within the house. She waited several seconds, then she ran her palms down her hips and turned to try to peek in the garage door windows. There were no cars there.

She studied the house next door. It looked shut up too, but the garage door stood open across the street, and a teenaged girl struggled with a large wheeled trash can.

Margaret hurried over. "Let me help with that."

The petite brunette eyed her a bit suspiciously but shrugged. "Thanks."

"I'm Margaret Ceradsky."

"Julie Scanfield."

"Hi, Julie. I'm from out of town, and I wanted to see Andrew Bartimus while I'm here. Do you have any idea where I could find him?"

"You don't know about—" Julie stopped and bit her lip.

Margaret straightened and studied the teen's face. She looked perplexed, and were those tears in her eyes?

"Know what?" Margaret asked, afraid she knew. Andrew was already dead. Rage engulfed her, and she clenched her hands, which trembled at her sides.

The girl whispered, "About Quintin?"

"No," Margaret said, her mind in confusion. Who was Quintin, and why was Julie so touched?

"Quintin died a few weeks ago," Julie sobbed. "I'm sorry, but I used to babysit with him and Quinthia, and I just can't believe he's gone."

The twins Susan mentioned, and one of them is dead.

"Oh, honey, how horrible for you," Margaret said. She laid her arm around the girl's shoulders and pulled her close. "It's horrible to lose someone you care about."

She held the sniffling teen for a few moments as she fought to control her own emotions of hurt, anger, and grief. Once she trusted her voice she asked, "Was he sick long?"

Julie nodded. "He and Quinthia both had leukemia. The treatments seemed to help Quinthia, but nothing they did ever helped Quintin." Julie blew her nose. "Now, they're both gone, and I really miss them."

"They're both gone?"

"Yeah. The day after the funeral, Mr. Bartimus put Quinthia in his van and drove off. We haven't seen either one of them since then."

"How long ago was that?"

"Three weeks." Julie dabbed her eyes. "The kids were so cute. I miss them both something awful."

Margaret nodded. "I'm sure you do, honey. Do you have any idea where Andy went?"

"Not really. He didn't talk about much except the kids. I worried about him."

"Why?" Margaret couldn't imagine a reason to worry about Andy. He deserved whatever ill should fall upon him.

"He worked so hard, and he always came downstairs and played with the kids, and fed them, and gave them their baths. He even read to them for hours and hours. He went to the library two or three times a week. He never did anything for himself."

"Lots of women do things like that for their families everyday," Margaret said, feeling no sympathy at all.

"Yeah, but Mr. Bartimus looked so sad and tired all the time."

"If he left, who's running his business?"

Julie frowned. "I don't know, probably nobody. He worked for himself out of the house."

"Maybe he went to his parents' house to get some help, do you think?"

"I don't know. He never mentioned anyone else. He was so concerned about the twins, I think if there was anyone else, he would have asked for help a lot before now."

"Probably, but then sometimes a man's pride keeps him from asking until he's desperate."

"Yeah, but I think if he could have, he would have asked sooner. Mr. Bartimus was sick a lot himself."

Margaret couldn't control her anger any longer. "Not as sick as that poor baby. He should have thought about death and its horrors before he had any children."

She turned and stalked back to her car, refusing to turn and look at the shock she knew would be registered on Julie's face.

Margaret had not planned to stay in Texas more than today, but it was several hours before her return flight would leave. She thought about how abruptly she had lashed out at Julie and, for a moment, felt a sense of shame, but it was too late to worry about that now.

Margaret's whole body felt warm, and her head ached. Her blood pressure must be skyrocketing.

I have to calm down. It won't help if I have a stroke.

She forced her mind to focus on driving toward downtown Dallas. She pulled into a shopping center where she spotted a tiny cafe. She went in and ordered coffee and a piece of coconut pie, which was advertised as homemade. When it came, she gave a contented sigh.

"I haven't seen real meringue on restaurant pies in years."

"Really? We do well to keep ours long enough to cool before they're sold out."

"I can see why," Margaret said when she eyed the two-inch-high foam.

She ate the pie and sipped her coffee while she planned her next step. Was there anything more she could do here in Texas to find Andy? Check the phone book? She already knew Andy's address, and from an earlier try, she knew his phone number was unlisted.

But maybe his business would be there. She forgot to ask Julie the name of Andy's company, and she sure couldn't go back now. There would be too many questions to answer.

Margaret motioned for the waitress.

"Was everything okay?" the lady asked as she placed Margaret's ticket on the table.

"Oh, yes. The pie's outstanding," Margaret said. "I'd like a little more coffee, though, and do you have a Corinth phone book I could use?" Maybe Andy's business would be listed with the house address.

"Sure," the waitress said. "I'll be right back."

True to her word, she soon handed Margaret the requested book. It was the Lake Dallas directory and it held listings for Corinth, Lake Dallas, and several other suburbs, as well as D/FW airport.

Great, Margaret thought. *I wonder how many computer consultants there are in all those places?*

She thumbed the book open to the yellow pages and flipped to the computer listings. There were fewer than half a dozen. She quickly copied the phone numbers into a small notebook she pulled from her purse. She thanked the cashier and paid the bill.

"Is there a public phone anywhere close?"

"Sure. There's a couple down the mall about half way."

Margaret found the phones and fed one her quarters. A man at the last place on her list spoke in typical Texas drawl. "Shore, I know Andy. Me and him worked on a couple o' projects. Good man, and he really knows his stuff."

Margaret preferred to keep Andy on the villain shelf in her mind.

The man went on. "Is he doing some job for you?"

"No. I'm an acquaintance of his from Kansas City, and I just thought I'd look him up while I'm here. A neighbor says he hasn't been home for a week or two. Do you happen to have any ideas about where he might have gone?"

"He's not home?"

"Not since the day after his son's funeral, according to a neighbor."

"Yeah, that was the last I saw him, too. Man, I felt bad for him. I can't even think about losin' one of my youngun's without comin' unglued. Somethin' like that makes you really step back and realize how blessed you are."

"Yes," Margaret murmured, wishing she was blessed enough to be thankful for her daughter's well-being, but it was too late for that now.

"Look, I don't mean to be rude, but my plane leaves in a few hours, and if I'm going to see Andy, I need to hustle."

"Oh, yeah, sure. I don't know of any family he has around here, and he sure didn't have time to make many friends."

"Do you know whether his wife's folks live here? I think he got married in Kansas, but I don't know where her parents are."

"Me neither. I . . . wait a minute. Andy did mention at the funeral that Quintin is buried next to his grandma."

"Did you notice the last name on the marker?"

"I'm sorry, ma'am, but I didn't."

"Could you tell me how to get to the cemetery?"

"It must be pretty important for you to see Andy if you're gonna go there."

"It is."

"Where are you? I'm not much good at givin' directions, but I know my way around. I could drive you there."

Margaret debated. She hated to impose on him, but if she didn't get some information, her whole trip would be wasted.

She told the man the street address and the color and model of her rental car.

"I'll be there in five minutes."

Margaret recognized the man by the computer logos on his van.

"Get in. The cemetery isn't far from here, and I'll drop you back by when you're done."

"I could follow you."

"No need. Hop in," he insisted.

Margaret walked around the white van and climbed in.

"Howdy, ma'am. I'm Hank Arnold." Margaret liked Hank on sight. He wore tan slacks, a beige shirt, and a bolo tie with a silver bull's head slide.

"Margaret Ceradsky."

"Well, hang on. If you're in a hurry, I'm just your man."

Margaret feared for her life as Hank weaved through traffic on the city streets, but at last they passed through the cemetery entrance.

"Andy must have gone to his folks' place. Quintin's grave is just over this little rise."

Hank pointed, then came to help Margaret out and lead her to the correct spot.

There were still dried up floral arrangements spread over the mounded dirt, and a small metal marker read:

QUINTIN BARTIMUS

TWO YEARS OLD

AND WITH THE ANGELS

Margaret resented her mental image of Angela holding a baby Quintin in heaven. Of course, the child was not responsible for his father's sins, but how could Angela be expected to accept the offspring of someone who cost her life itself? The question troubled Margaret, for angry as she was, she realized that without forgiveness in her heart, Angela could not be in heaven to even try to accept Quintin. She didn't want to think about it anymore.

"Which side is the grandmother's?" she asked Hank.

The lanky Texan strode to the left in his ornately decorated boots.

"Over here, I think, but I'm not sure. The marker on the right is Quinella's, and this double one says Pepe and Consuelo Sanchez, so this must be it."

Margaret gazed at the engraving. The Sanchezes died on the same date. That was odd.

"Quinella was Andy's wife?"

"Yes, ma'am. She died when the twins were born, and Andy put her here, then when Quintin passed away, Andy put him in the spot he'd bought for himself. He never figured on buryin' his young'un first."

"No. We usually don't, do we?" Margaret knew exactly how bitter it was to bury a child, and she was glad Andrew had been forced to taste the gall of anguish she had borne. It was poetic justice that he had buried two people to her one.

"I didn't realize Quinella was Hispanic."

"Yes, ma'am, a real beauty. Tiny and delicate like. Andy said her family goes back hundreds of years in this area."

"So she was from here in Corinth?"

"As far as I know."

"Did she have any brothers and sisters?"

"I don't rightly know, ma'am."

"Sanchez must be a common name down here. Even in Kansas City I'd probably find several families listed in the phone book."

"I reckon, sort of like Smith or Jones." Hank smiled and brushed his hand through the lock of golden blonde hair that had blown across his forehead.

He had gone out of his way to help, but frustration overwhelmed her. What did she do now?

"Well, it looks like I go back to Kansas City without seeing Andy this trip."

"I'm sure sorry, ma'am. If I knew where else to look, I'd shore do it for you."

"I know, and I appreciate it, but I guess you should take me back to my car for now."

Chapter Thirteen

At the shopping center, Margaret thanked Hank, then went back into the cafe and asked to use their phone directory again. To her surprise, there were only four Sanchezes listed in Corinth, so she looked in the Denton section and found eleven more. She went back to the public phones and spent the next forty-five minutes calling all the Sanchezes on her list. None of them were related to Quinella Bartimus.

Margaret looked at her watch. One P.M. She still had six hours before her flight left. A visit to city hall and the public records might give her a lead, if she found a knowledgeable clerk to help her. She drove into Dallas and found the city hall. Inside she asked where she could go to find marriage license and death certificate records. A lady pointed her to a nearby door, "Try there." Margaret entered and saw a long counter.

A short, kinky-haired redhead asked, "May ah help you, ma'am?"

Margaret smiled. "Yes, please. I'm looking for some family records and was wondering if I could get copies of a marriage certificate and death certificates for Pepe and Consuelo Sanchez."

"Do you know the dates of death or the marriage?"

"I know the date of death." Margaret pulled the notebook from her purse. "But I don't know a marriage date."

"Do you have their Social Security numbers?"

"No. I'm sorry, I don't."

"Well, I'll see what I can do with the dates of death. Maybe we can work backward from computer records."

"That would be wonderful," Margaret said. "I'm particularly interested in locating any living children."

"Have a seat over there, and I'll see what I can bring up."

Margaret waited almost thirty minutes before the woman waved at her.

"Ah think ah have what you want. Sometimes it takes a while to get all the pieces for you genealogy searchers, but we try to please. Pepe and Consuelo Sanchez were married here in Dallas in 1930. They had three children: Quinella, Roberto, and Vincenzia. Quinella died two years ago. I only have birth records for Roberto and Vincenzia. Pepe and Consuelo were both killed in a car crash."

The woman handed Margaret the computer print out.

"Thank you so much. I never dreamed you could find so much information so quickly."

The woman smiled. "Computers are wonderful, if they work."

In the lobby, Margaret scanned her phone listings. No Robertos or Vincenzias there. She headed to a nearby phone booth to check out the Dallas listings. No luck.

She glanced at her watch. She would have to hurry to get the car returned and make her flight.

Julie said Andy was sick. Margaret had to locate him soon. He must not die before she charged him with his sin, but how was she going to find him?

It was late when Margaret arrived home, but Cat ran to greet her and wrap herself around Margaret's legs.

"Hi, pest. You missed me, huh?" Margaret set her purse on the floor and plopped in the pink rose-covered easy chair next to the window. Cat sprang into her lap and reared up to lick Margaret's neck. Margaret smiled and pushed Cat back down onto her lap.

"You can sit here, but no kisses!" She stroked her hand down the kitten's back several times and tried to unwind. Maybe she could sleep in tomorrow before she started her weekend routine of laundry and grocery shopping.

Fat chance, she chided herself. She knew she would never rest until she found Andrew Bartimus, but she was out of ideas about where to look.

The next morning Micah called. "May I come and get you for services this morning?"

Margaret groaned. "I don't know. I'm not even awake yet."

"Oh, come on. Can you be ready in an hour? There's someone I want you to meet."

Margaret smothered the mutter she knew would burst forth if she wasn't careful. She decided she might as well go. It might be good for her. She wasn't having any luck finding Andy, and she needed something to take her mind off her failure.

True to his word, Micah arrived in exactly one hour.

"Hi. You look great!" he said in admiration of Margaret's light lavender suit.

"Thank you. This is one of my favorite outfits," she said as she pushed down the warm feeling that squeezed at her heart.

At the church, Micah ushered her into the auditorium and seated her only a few rows from the front. In a few minutes, Ed and a young woman with a baby and LaMont and his friends came and sat beside her.

"Hi. It's good to see you here," Ed said. "I want you to meet Kathy, and you've already met Desmond."

"Hello, Kathy, and hello to you, too, Desmond." The baby drooled through his toothless smile, and his dark eyes sparkled with glee.

Kathy laughed. "He never meets a stranger. We're both glad you're here."

"Thank you for sitting with me. I feel rather awkward all alone." Margaret admired Kathy's rich mahogany complexion, her warm, guileless, and unmistakably friendly smile.

Kathy wriggled the diaper bag onto the floor and positioned Desmond more comfortably.

The service passed quickly, and Margaret was ashamed that she could not remember much of what Micah said, for Desmond started fussing just as Micah stood to preach, and Margaret took the baby and entertained him throughout the remainder of the service. She hoped Micah wouldn't quiz her later.

He did come to collect her and escorted her to the back of the building. "I have to greet everyone before I can leave, but it shouldn't take too long," he told her in a near whisper.

LaMont grabbed her arm. "I'll just take her out and show her my kites," he said.

Micah nodded, and Margaret tried to look at him for direction as LaMont dragged her across the vestibule. Did Micah want her to go, or did he want her to stay with him? She couldn't tell, but decided he must not want her beside him. After all, she could be an embarrassment to him, since she wasn't a member of his congregation. Someone might put the wrong connotation on her presence at his side, and he was the preacher after all. He had to protect his reputation. Not that he had done anything wrong, but preachers had to be concerned about even the appearance of evil. She'd read that one evening as she thumbed through her Bible.

LaMont tugged even harder. "Come on, Margaret, I want to show you something."

She followed, but obviously not as quickly as LaMont would have liked. She watched the animation on LaMont's face. He pulled something from the trunk Ed had popped open. "I wanted to see if you could help me fix a tear in this kite."

"Kite? I don't know—"

"You gotta see these kites in the air, Margaret. They're awesome."

Margaret looked at the slender tube LaMont held. It didn't look like anything associated with kites she had ever seen before.

Her experience with them was the paper variety the kids bought at the toy stores. She instinctively knew by the case LaMont carried this was a whole different class of sport from her few childhood experiences.

"Oh, I think I should pass," she said. "I have drapes to finish, and time's flying."

LaMont feigned a pout. "But Micah said you would probably help us repair one of the kites the guys tore a couple of weeks ago."

Just then, Micah rushed across the parking lot to join them.

"Wait up, Margaret. I wanted to talk to you about Saturday afternoon, but I see LaMont has probably already said something."

Margaret smiled at Micah. She couldn't help noticing how athletic he was. He looked so handsome, and she wanted to reach out and brush the errant gray lock from his forehead as she had often done for George.

But she didn't.

"Yes, he mentioned repairs. I don't know much about patching paper."

Micah and LaMont both laughed and Margaret looked from one to the other.

"Here," LaMont said. "Let me show you." He began to unscrew the end of the tube he held.

Another man approached, "Hi, LaMont. You gonna assess the damage?"

LaMont glanced up. "Yeah, I was comin' to look for you when I run into Margaret and Micah here."

The man extended his hand to Micah and openly surveyed Margaret. "Hello, Margaret," he said around Micah's shoulder. "I'm Bruce Jacobson, and I'm very happy to meet you."

Margaret smiled into the man's true blue eyes and couldn't help the soft flutter she recognized as physical attraction, but she could tell from the man's tone he was a flirt, and probably was happily married and had eight or ten grandchildren. She suddenly realized she must be healing at least a bit if she could notice how attractive a man was, let alone two men in less than two minutes.

Micah turned to Margaret, "Watch yourself. Bruce loves pretty women, and he's an incorrigible flirt, but he's a good man in spite of himself."

Bruce extended his hand to Margaret and held hers a moment too long for her comfort. She didn't know why she felt so ill at ease. The man was quite attractive, the flirtatious manner was obviously in fun, and he seemed nice enough, but her feelings toward him held none of the warmth she felt when Micah spoke.

"Bruce is responsible for all this kite flying business. He introduced the guys to flying last year."

LaMont, by this time, had assembled his kite. "Ain't this somethin'?" he asked when he held it up.

She looked and was indeed amazed. The kite spanned almost six feet, was made of fluorescent fabric, and it arched over some sort of framework that looked like plastic. The black and bright-pink colors all but screamed at her.

"Hector's got torn last week, and we have a competition Saturday. Micah thought you might help us out."

He opened his eyes in a universal expression of supplication, and she couldn't help responding.

"Okay, so what do I use to repair it?"

"It's a special nylon, and I can get everything you need at Wind Wizards," LaMont explained.

"What's that?" Margaret asked.

"The kite store. They have everything we need."

Bruce spoke up. "Have you decided what you need? We could all go to lunch, and you and I could run out and pick up the supplies. If you fellows do well in Saturday's competition, I'll want to buy one of those big hexagon numbers next. You boys could have a ball with one of those."

LaMont's eyes grew huge. "You got any idea how much one of those babies costs?"

"Sure. It's only money, and you guys are good!"

"I've seen those in the mags, but I ain't never actually seen one up close. I'd do almost anything to get my hands on one of them." LaMont turned to Margaret. "You gotta get this thing fixed up real good!"

Margaret laughed. "Well, if you get everything I need, I'll do my best."

Bruce grabbed her elbow and started toward a nearby car. "Then, it's off to lunch, and to Wind Wizards."

Margaret resisted. "Wait a minute. I can't go. You fellows can go on without me. I have some things to tend at home this afternoon."

She glanced at Micah for support, and she was surprised at the look of bewilderment on his face before he spoke.

"Perhaps you could go to lunch, and I can drive you back here to get your car, and Bruce and LaMont can go do their shopping."

Margaret hesitated. She had intended to go home and work on

the church draperies this afternoon. She knew it was Sunday and it could be considered a day of rest, but she had a deadline drawing closer by the minute. Even if she rested all day, she knew her mind would race with thoughts of Angela, and what they would be doing if Angela were alive. Those thoughts would then lead to Andrew Bartimus. No, rest was not hers, but work gave her a sense of accomplishment and the only measure of peace she supposed she would ever again experience.

She knew she had paused an inordinate amount of time when Micah asked, "Don't you feel well?"

Margaret smiled at the concern in his voice. Dear Micah, the man who cared so deeply for the people around him.

"I'm fine," she said. "It's just that I have some things to do, and I'm assuming by later this afternoon you three will be on my doorstep with a mending job to be done."

LaMont shuffled his feet and looked contrite. "Hey, if it's gonna be a problem, we can get Kathy to do it." He glanced up at Margaret. "But she ain't so good with a needle."

"Oh, no, LaMont," Margaret protested. "I didn't mean that. All I'm saying is, I don't have time to do it all, and since I want to mend the kite for you, I need to grab a quick lunch and tackle my other projects before you get there. Don't you dare bother Kathy and that darling baby, or I'll really be upset."

LaMont's grin warmed her when he said, "Okay. We'll see you later this afternoon. You gotta go with us to the competition on Saturday. So, save that afternoon for us."

Margaret glanced at Micah, and he nodded. "You won't be sorry. It's a spectacular sight to see all those kites in the sky."

Chapter Fourteen

Margaret stood at her kitchen window on Saturday morning and drank in the soft pink, yellow, and orange glow in the eastern sky. It would be a great kite day.

She sipped her coffee and contemplated the outing before her. Bruce had promised to buy a huge hexagon kite for them to use as a team once LaMont and his friends developed their skill enough.

She marveled at Bruce's generosity, but she was certain it was a direct result of Micah's influence. She thought long about how none of this would have happened if Micah had not first forgiven Ed and become involved in LaMont's life. She could see the good being done here with Ed, LaMont, and his friends, and even with Bruce.

She began to get at least an inkling of the meaning of the Scripture that says "all things work together for good to those who love God." She could see that happening with these people, but she knew in her heart there was nothing good to be found in Angela's death.

She ground her teeth and turned from the window. Better to think about the kite show and not dwell on Angela.

She rushed to her room to dress and wondered what would be appropriate for a kite fly. Thinking of all the brilliant colors she'd seen in LaMont's kite catalog, she chose a bright-red pant suit and a navy-and-white scarf. She put on clunky gold earrings and a spritz of a floral-blend cologne, and finished just as Micah rang the doorbell.

"Oh my, how sporty you look," he said when he stepped back to survey the full picture. His broad smile and the little crinkles around his eyes said even more than his words, and Margaret felt a flutter around her heart.

Careful girl, she told herself, but she smiled back and picked up the small purse that held a few necessities.

Cat wrapped herself around Margaret's leg. "Shoo—go to your bed," Margaret scolded. Cat blinked, lifted her tail in disdain, and sauntered toward the kitchen.

"Honestly, she can be such a nuisance, but she is company."

Micah chuckled. "You're just a big softy."

Margaret shrugged and pulled the front door closed. "Where is this thing to be held?"

Micah seated her in the car. "Over by the Boardwalk Shopping Center. There's a huge open field out there."

Margaret knew it would take only a few minutes to reach their destination, so she decided to appease her curiosity quickly.

"Micah, what makes Bruce so willing to spend the time and money he does on LaMont and his friends? I nearly swallowed my tongue when I saw the prices on those kites."

"They are expensive, although they don't necessarily have to be. Some of the younger kids fly the toy-store variety and manage to have a lot of fun. But to answer your question, Bruce loves being around the guys. The kites and the scholarships are minor expenses to him. He says the teens keep him young and help him keep his sanity."

"Teens? That could be debatable," Margaret joked.

"I know, but he used to be a workaholic, and it cost him his family. His daughter had an affair, which broke his heart. She did marry her baby's father, but that only compounded an already bad situation."

"What do you mean?"

"The boy she married refused to work, and he beat her, until one day she packed herself and the baby up and just disappeared. Nobody knows where she is."

"Oh, poor Bruce."

"Yes, but it didn't stop there. He and his son got into a huge brawl one night, and his son apparently lambasted Bruce with all his sins, real and imagined, and he stormed out of the house and joined the Army. Bruce has heard from him only once, and that was through a service news release sent to the Gladstone paper about him completing a specialized flying course and his subsequent promotion."

"How sad. Has he never called or written?"

"Not once. It nearly broke Bruce, but about then his wife finally convinced him to come to church. It took a while for him to let his wall of anger down enough for the Word to pierce his heart, but when it did, he put on the full armor of God, swift and sure. He's been a one-man benevolence committee ever since, but LaMont and the guys are his special love."

Micah glanced at her and Margaret forced a smile. "Don't worry. He can afford it, and I've seen him grow so quickly I almost had to jump back out of the way. It's amazing how God's love can transform people, and how once one person grows, they seem to pull other people up with them."

They topped a small knoll and Margaret gasped. "Oh, look! They started without us, and aren't the kites beautiful?"

Micah pulled into a grassy area where other cars were already parked. "I always enjoy watching."

They walked the perimeter of the field until they spotted Bruce, Ed, LaMont, Hector, and Yin Ling. Bruce rushed to meet them and took Margaret's elbow to lead them to where the boys worked.

Margaret noticed the boys all wore matching turquoise shirts. "I assume the shirts are compliments of Bruce."

"Of course," Micah said. "They're a team."

She looked around and noticed other clusters of people in various matched sets of clothing. Bruce certainly would want the boys to feel equally as well-equipped as any other team.

She turned back to LaMont and his friends and saw each one had assembled a large kite, all in different colors but the same geometric pattern. Margaret's curiosity got the best of her when she saw the boys attach the kites together with a length of some sort of line between each one.

"Why are they doing that?"

Bruce waved his hand toward the group. "Because they are one of the best flying teams out here, and they're going to show this crowd how to fly a train."

Margaret surveyed the field and gave a coy smile. "No way. No tracks, and there isn't a kite in the world big enough to lift a train engine."

Bruce and all the boys laughed.

"Not that kind of train," Ed said. "We hook these kites together and send them up in a line, or train, and fly them all off one line. It's not easy, but we do it all the time."

"That's because they're the best," Bruce said. "We're gonna send up seven today, because you're here, and you can help hold one for lift-off."

"Me?" she asked in surprise. "I don't know anything about how to do that."

"It's a piece of cake," Hector said. "You'll hold the last one, and when we get the others going, they'll lift it, and by that time, the lead man can run back and help you!"

Margaret cast Bruce and Micah skeptical glances, but Micah nodded, so she decided they certainly knew better than she what would or would not work.

"We saved the pink and black one for you," LaMont said as he hooked the connecting line to the last kite.

Hector shouted, "We're ready to launch off. Come and let me show you how to hold this."

Margaret hesitated, so Yin Ling came and took her hand. "It won't bite you, and the nylon's tough. It's a whiz."

Hector came over and offered pointers, and Yin Ling showed her slants, talked about lift, and how taut to keep the connecting lines. Margaret wasn't convinced this would work, but she decided she couldn't let the guys down, so she listened intently.

"Okay, LaMont," Bruce said, "lead us off, and let's get these things in the air so people can see how tough we are on the flying field."

Several minutes later, Margaret gasped for breath from running several yards, but she shaded her eyes and leaned her head back to see seven kites flying, one behind the other, high overhead.

It was one of the most beautiful things she had ever seen. She looked across the field as LaMont held the lead line, and the other boys ran to lift slack line off the grass and help with control.

Micah walked back to her. "Well, what do you think?"

"It's amazing. I've never seen anything like it, especially since there's hardly any breeze. How do they do that?"

"It does take a good bit of practice, and Bruce has worked hours with them, but wait 'til you see the figure competition tonight. They'll fly kites in specific patterns, and there'll be lights on the struts. It's absolutely beautiful."

"I can't imagine anything more spectacular than this."

But she was wrong. As the afternoon progressed, box kites, Japanese kites, and windsock kites in various whimsical shapes flew across the field.

Margaret accepted the folding chaise lounge Bruce offered and went to sit beneath the camping canopy he had erected on the edge of the field.

"Here, have a soda," he offered from a nearby cooler. "Just sit here and watch. I'm going to run some drinks out to the boys. I'll be right back."

Margaret opened the cold can and sipped, barely able to tear her gaze from the dancing kites overhead.

Micah came and dropped onto a chair next to her.

"Whew! It gets warm out there." He reached for a soda and opened it. "Are you enjoying yourself?"

"Yes, very much," Margaret said.

She turned, and her gaze locked with Micah's. She hesitated, swallowed, and said softly, "Thank you for inviting me. I haven't enjoyed anything this much in a long time."

"Good." He reached out and patted her hand, "We'll do it again, soon."

Her hand radiated a lovely sensation straight to her heart. *Get a grip, woman. Micah's not for you, or more like it, you're not for him. You'd never qualify as a preacher's wife.*

Her own thoughts startled her, for she realized how ugly the attributes she recognized in herself truly were, but she could not turn her feelings off. She knew she should, but she just couldn't.

The group brought their kites down gently, much to Margaret's amazement, and carried them to the canopied shade. Bruce told the boys to case up their kites, and then turned to Micah and Margaret. "The night fly won't start for a couple of hours, so we're all going to dinner, my treat, and we'll come back, and the boys will really mesmerize Margaret."

"Ed, you and LaMont can ride with me and Margaret," Micah said, "and we'll follow the others."

At a nearby restaurant, they chattered in excitement while they waited to be seated. The boys discussed successful strategies and plans for the night flight.

The lobby of the restaurant became quite crowded as they waited, but the lively conversation was enjoyable and kept the wait from being unpleasant.

"You shoulda seen that guy's rig. It barely had a wingspan this big," Yin Ling said as he swung his arms out to demonstrate and accidentally struck a young man standing nearby.

"Say, man, I'm sorry," Yin Ling rushed to say. "I guess I'm too excited."

The man turned, looked at Yin Ling up and down, and snarled. "Don't you never touch me again, chink." He pulled his shoulders back and straightened to his full height in order to tower over Yin Ling's five-foot-five frame.

LaMont pulled Yin Ling back. "Wait a minute. He said he was sorry. Just chill, man."

"Who you talkin' to, nigger? It shore ain't me you're tryin' to boss 'round, now is it?" the man sneered.

LaMont doubled his fists before Ed grabbed his arm and growled, "Let it go. Let's get out of here. Don't be stupid, man. He doesn't know any better, but you do. Come on."

Bruce forged an opening in the crowd, Micah caught the hostess's attention and motioned they were leaving, and the group rushed out.

The insolent man called to them, "And stay out. This here's a place for respectable folks!"

Micah and Bruce conferred quickly, and they drove to another restaurant down the street.

Once they were seated, Micah spoke. "Yin Ling, I'm so sorry that happened. Unfortunately, many people have never experienced God's love, so they don't love themselves, and that keeps them from being able to love other people."

"No sweat, man. He's just ignorant. Let's forget it."

"We will, except for one more thing. LaMont, I've seen you take a lot more than that when someone was calling you names, and I understand how much deeper it cuts when someone attacks a friend, but we still have to love them and walk away."

"I know, but he made me really mad! Man, Yin Ling's one of the best guys in the whole world, and that jerk had no right to talk like that!"

"You're right on all counts, but getting violent wouldn't change his mind, and it only makes a bad situation worse."

"I know, and I'm sorry. I promise I'll work on it."

"Good. Now, let's eat this marvelous meal and get back to the field."

Later that evening, Margaret watched the tiny lights dart around the sky to the beat of music that poured out of some unseen boom box. Several kites danced in unison to the beautiful classical piece. She was lulled into an ecstatic tranquility she knew she hadn't experienced since before Angela became ill. She soaked in the languorous serenity like a wilted flower drinking up water, until her soul swelled to overflowing.

A few minutes later, the calm shattered around her when a car sped up, stopped opposite the canopy, and a man stepped out and shouted, "Hey, nigger. Ain't nobody gettin' by with callin' me stupid."

Margaret watched in horror when she saw the man lift a gun and point it at Ed; then she heard the deafening sound of a shot.

Chapter Fifteen

Margaret didn't remember much after that until they arrived at the hospital. Because of being clergy, Micah was allowed into the emergency room. Margaret went to a nearby waiting room and found a seat. All she could do was pray, and she didn't feel she knew enough to be able to do that, and even if she could, what made her think God would listen to her now?

A few minutes later, Margaret heard footsteps running down the hall in her direction. Opening her arms, she went to meet Kathy.

The panicked young woman flew to her and sobbed. "Have you heard anything yet?"

"No. Micah's inside, and I guess LaMont must be, too."

"LaMont?"

"Yes. He rode in the ambulance and I haven't seen him, so I suppose he's still in there."

"They wouldn't let me in," Kathy sobbed.

"I know. But they need the space to give Ed the best care possible."

Kathy twisted a tissue into a tiny knot. "Why did this have to happen? Ed's worked so hard, and he's turned into a really good man. Why—?"

"I can't answer that. I've been wondering, too."

Margaret led Kathy into the waiting room and to a chair. "Who has the baby?"

Kathy's nervous little laugh startled Margaret. "Bruce and Hector and Yin Ling are watching him. He may have his diaper on his ears when I get home." Her smile faded and she added, "If I get home."

Margaret moved to hug Kathy and she gently rocked her as she murmured reassurances. "He'll be fine . . . They're working hard in there . . . They have all the best equipment . . . He'll be okay, you'll see."

Almost an hour later, Micah entered the room. Kathy and Margaret jumped up to meet him.

"Is he—?" Kathy started, then froze when she saw the grim look on Micah's face.

He motioned the two women back to chairs and he perched on one opposite them. He reached out and took Kathy's hand. Then he spoke softly. "He's still alive. He's lost a lot of blood. His is a rare type, so they've linked him and LaMont for a direct transfusion. They've taken them up to surgery. The bullet seems to be lodged near Ed's spine."

"Oh, God," Kathy cried. Tears coursed down her cheeks, and Margaret's hand ached from Kathy's grip. But she couldn't pull away. She knew it was probably the only way Kathy could maintain any semblance of composure.

"We can move to the waiting room up there, and the doctor will report to us as soon as they finish," Micah said.

They took the elevator to the surgical floor, and as they passed a telephone in the hall, Kathy said, "I should call Bruce."

She fumbled in her jean pockets for some coins.

Micah thrust forth a handful of change. "Here, and keep the extra. You may need to call again."

"Thanks," she said and went to place her call.

Margaret and Micah walked on to the waiting room, only a few steps down the hall.

"So?" she asked.

"Still pretty grim," Micah said. "All we can do is pray, and we need to do a lot of that."

Kathy came back and gave a weak smile. "Bruce says Desmond's asleep. He and the guys are watching television. They're going to spend the night."

"Good," Micah said. "Did you leave the phone number in case they need you?"

"Yes," Kathy said, "I did remember to do that."

They went to the waiting room and sat down before Micah said, "Kathy, we know God loves us and answers our prayers, but we have to talk to him and tell him our needs. Now's the time."

Kathy nodded and held out a hand to Micah and one to Margaret. They bowed their heads, but Micah said nothing for several long seconds. Margaret felt uncomfortable, then realized they were praying silently. Just as she began to try to organize her thoughts, Micah spoke:

> "Dear Father, we thank you for allowing us the privilege of prayer through Jesus. You know our fears and our concerns, but we ask you to bless the doctors who are ministering to Ed with enhanced skills, and give Ed the strength he needs to benefit from their work. Please grant Ed life and good health. Be with Kathy and give her the strength she's going to need to help him and to keep her family together. Help her brothers and sisters in the church to recognize her needs and to come to her aid. For all these blessings we thank you and praise your holy name. Amen."

Margaret sat perfectly still for a moment. Did Micah really believe all that stuff? Did he think God would just go "zappo-change-o!" and Ed would be fine? Her anger gurgled again. She swallowed and looked up. Kathy needed her, right now. She would puzzle through this prayer thing later.

In the wee hours of the morning, Micah nudged Margaret and woke her. She jolted upright when she realized the surgeon stood before them.

"I'm sorry it took us so long," he said. "Mr. Johnson is in recovery."

Margaret and Micah jumped to their feet and stood on either side of Kathy.

"He's alive," the surgeon said quietly, "but he's still in a good bit of danger."

Kathy moaned, and whispered, "Thank God he's alive."

"Yes," Micah said. "Hang on to that, Kathy. Don't forget God loves you both, no matter what happens."

Margaret felt her screaming muscles knot between her shoulders from flexed tension. How long had they sat, waiting to learn if Ed had survived? Four, five hours? She didn't know. But Ed was alive, and their prayers had been answered.

The doctor continued. "The bullet lodged very near the spine. I won't go into all the technicalities of the surgery, but if he recovers, it's almost certain he'll never be able to walk again. We're doing everything possible, but unfortunately, it may not be enough." He lifted his hands in a gesture of sympathy. "I'm sorry."

"No!" Kathy screamed. "No! He couldn't stand to be a cripple. He would rather die." She grabbed the surgeon's sleeve.

"Why didn't you let him die? He won't be able to stand it."

Micah took Kathy's arm and pulled her away. "Kathy? Kathy! Calm down. Be thankful this good man has used his skills to keep Ed with you and Desmond. Ed will learn to deal with whatever comes. But he needs you to be strong and help him. You've stayed beside him before. He needs you even more now."

Kathy slumped into Micah's arms and sobbed in desperation.

Margaret knew some of the hysterics were a release of the fear and frustration Kathy had forced down over the past several hours, but she also knew some of the fears Kathy expressed were real. How would Kathy cope without Ed's income? She couldn't help wondering where God was when all this happened.

Why hadn't they picked some other restaurant? Why had that hothead twisted Ed's admonishment to LaMont and decided Ed was calling him stupid? Why hadn't he accepted Yin Ling's apology? Margaret didn't understand, but she knew the whole situation was tragic, and it made her furious. She wanted to kick, scream, and hit someone.

"How long before I can see him?" Kathy asked the surgeon.

"He probably won't wake for several hours."

"Is there any chance at all he could be able to walk?" Micah asked.

Margaret and Kathy both turned to the doctor. *Please, God, let him say yes,* Margaret prayed.

The surgeon spread his hands. "I'm not sure. It could be several days before we know that." He turned to Kathy. "In all honesty, I don't see any way he could walk, but I've seen a few amazing cases defy all I know about medicine."

Kathy sank back in her chair and blotted her nose. The tears ran unabated. "Oh, God, what will we *do?*"

Margaret put her arms around Kathy and let her sob out her anguish.

The surgeon turned to Micah, "I'm truly sorry—you should probably all go home until tomorrow—or this afternoon."

He glanced at his watch and gave a wry smile because it was well past midnight. "Mr. Johnson won't rally for several hours, and we're keeping his brother until later this morning also, just to let him rest. We drew off quite a bit of his blood, and he'll feel a little weak for a while."

Micah nodded. "Thank you, doctor."

"If you have any questions, contact one of the nurses, and they'll either answer you or page me." With that, he turned and left the stunned little clutch to try to gather its wits and decide what to do next.

Micah dropped Kathy off at home, promised to meet her at the hospital at eight o'clock, then took Margaret home.

Margaret glanced at the glowing light on the dashboard clock. "That only gives you about three hours' sleep after you pull out travel time," she said.

"I know, but Kathy won't be able to rest, and she needs me."

He gave a little wave of resignation. "I've gone without sleep before."

"Should I meet you there?"

"I don't think you need to be there by eight, but if you wanted to come down later, I'm sure Kathy would appreciate it. She seems to have opened up to you."

Margaret cast a questioning glance, and Micah continued. "Kathy's kept herself distanced from the ladies at church. I think she feared being snubbed, both because of her race and Ed's background.

Many of the women have offered her invitations to do things, but Kathy's always remained aloof from any real relationships."

"I'm sure some of her fears were valid. People can be quite cruel at times."

"Ordinary people, yes, and I guess truth be known, even some Christians, but we have a great group at Liberty, and they wouldn't intentionally hurt Kathy or anyone else."

"That's good, but if I'm the one she's comfortable with, I'm the one who should be there for her."

"I appreciate that," Micah said, "and I'm sure Kathy will, too."

When they reached Margaret's driveway, a shiny white car with emergency lights on top waited for her return. Two huge men in rumpled suits stepped out of the car. "Margaret Ceradsky?" one asked.

"Yes."

"I'm Lt. Bill Henson, and this is Officer John Smith." He flipped out a badge, then replaced it in his breast pocket. "We need to talk to you about the shooting."

Micah opened his mouth to protest.

The officer interrupted. "I know she hasn't had much sleep but the longer we wait, the less likely we are to find him."

"It's okay, Micah. You go on home and sleep. I'll meet you at the hospital as soon as I wake, later this morning."

Micah hesitated.

"We won't keep her long. We just need a few more details. We've picked up a guy for questioning, based on other witnesses' descriptions of the car, but we need Mrs. Ceradsky's information to confirm the ID."

"Do you really think you have the right guy?" Micah asked.

Officer Smith nodded. "This isn't the first time this guy's lost his temper, except he graduated from fists to a gun this time."

"It'll be good to get him off the streets," Micah said as he turned to Margaret. "Are you sure you don't need anything else?"

"I'm sure. You get some rest."

Micah nodded and went to his car.

"Let's go inside," Margaret said to the officers.

When she opened the door, Cat wrapped herself around Margaret's ankles and yowled pitifully.

"Oh, dear, I forgot all about you. Excuse me a moment while I feed her, or we won't have any peace at all." Margaret led the men to the living room. "Have a seat. I'll be right back."

She rushed to the kitchen and shook some cat chow into Cat's dish, then filled the water bowl. It gave her a few minutes to compose her thoughts.

She didn't want to be involved in any of this. If these men did find who shot Ed, she would have to testify. She didn't have time for all that. She had drapes to make, and an investigation of her own to conduct, and now it looked like she would be spending a lot of time with Kathy.

On the other hand, if these men didn't have the right man, Margaret had no doubt LaMont and his friends would start their own search. She shuddered at the thought of how far that could go awry.

She took a deep breath, stiffened her resolve to answer all the questions as truthfully as she could, and headed to the living room.

Thirty minutes later, Lt. Henson folded away his notebook. "You've pretty well confirmed our suspicions. We should be able to charge this guy today. We'll call you to come down for the lineup as soon as we can set it up."

Margaret nodded. "I'm going to sleep awhile, then go back to the hospital. If I'm not here, you should be able to get me, or Micah, there."

"Isn't he a preacher?" Officer Smith asked.

"Yes, why?"

"Today's Sunday. I figured he might have to preach this morning." Margaret gasped. "He does!—but not until eleven. He was going to meet Kathy at eight, but he'll have to leave no later than ten-thirty to be at church on time. If he goes to Bible study, he'll have to leave by nine-fifteen."

"Where will you be?"

"I'm not sure. You'll just have to call all those places. I'll be with Kathy."

Margaret had no special ties to the church, except for Micah and Ed's family. She couldn't imagine Kathy leaving Ed's side, but then, if she believed all that stuff Micah said in his prayer this morning, she just might.

Margaret escorted the officers to the door, then went to her bed. Why was sleep always so elusive when you needed it most? She still hadn't learned how to sleep fast.

Thoughts of Kathy and Desmond being without Ed's support saddened her. She was sure the young couple barely coped with Ed's salary as a janitor. How would they survive without even that much, especially with the hospital bills added to their already strained budget?

She flipped over to her left side and punched her pillow, then lay still, searching for sleep. Her thoughts raced again. If Ed was permanently crippled, he would never be able to contribute to the family's support. Poor Kathy.

Margaret willed her mind blank. Then consciously, she forced her body to relax, one limb at a time. As her body grew heavy, she knew she would drift off soon, and she welcomed the refreshment she needed so badly.

She awoke with a start to the telephone ringing. She groaned, but reached for the obnoxious instrument.

"Hello."

"Margaret, I'm sorry, but it's Micah. I'm at the hospital, and I have to get to the church. Bruce and the boys are at Kathy's house, and I guess Desmond is out of formula. They need somebody to take them some and show them how to prepare it."

Margaret glanced at the clock. Nine. She shouldn't feel so groggy once she got up and started moving. "I'll go right away. What brand?"

"What?"

"What brand of formula does Desmond use?"

"Oh—I don't know. Hold on."

A few seconds later he said, "Similac with iron."

"Fine. I'll leave as soon as I can get dressed."

"Thanks. I'll try to see you right after church."

"I don't know where I'll be. Are Bruce and the guys staying with Desmond, or do I need to?"

"I don't know. You'll have to work that out with them. Let me give you the phone number here in case you need to talk to Kathy."

Margaret took down the number before Micah said, "I'll come back here right after church."

"Fine," Margaret said. She re-cradled the receiver and swung her feet out of bed.

Her anger surged again. Why were vile men able to cause such chaos in other people's lives? Ed's shooter, Andrew Bartimus, and men like them lived violently, and they deserved to be treated violently. Was this God's way of punishing Ed? Margaret shook off the idea. God didn't punish people who had converted. Did He? Ed had made a new beginning, but not these other men. They certainly had not repented. She hoped the police really had Ed's attacker, and as soon as she had time, she intended to start her search for Andy again.

People like him and Ed's attacker should not be allowed to go unpunished.

The next few days were a blur of hours at the hospital with Kathy, then hours sitting with Desmond, since Bruce had to return to work. Of course, LaMont and his friends couldn't help. They were still in school.

Micah assured Margaret the drapes she needed to complete could wait. If they didn't get done in time for the homecoming, as originally planned, it would not be the end of the world. Kathy's needs came first.

"I'm just thankful you're willing to be so supportive of her, and she's able to accept it from you," Micah said.

Margaret was glad, too, but she fretted over the young couple's financial needs.

One afternoon Margaret sank wearily in the flower-covered chair and stroked Cat's sleepy head while she rested and contemplated all Micah had told her. She feared she would never be able to reconcile it all in her mind. She had a deep need to strike out at someone or something, anything would do. She just needed to vent some of her pent up frustration. But watching Micah and listening to all he said about forgiveness slowly began to sink in. Maybe, just maybe, she needed to lay aside her rage and get on with her own life. She jumped when the phone rang.

"Mrs. Ceradsky? This is Cliff Hunter. I know where you can find Andrew Bartimus."

Chapter Sixteen

*M*argaret gripped the arms of the chair. "What did you say?"

"I know where good ol' Andy is hidin', and you can know, too, for a mere five hundred green backs."

"I don't have that kind of cash," Margaret choked out. *And I don't want to know anymore,* she told herself before she spoke again. "You mistook me for somebody with money."

"Oh, come on, lady. You made a special trip down here to nose around and you tell me you ain't willin' to spend a lousy five hundred dollars to find your man? I mean, I didn't buy that flimsy story about a party. Nobody goes to the trouble you did for some party."

"You're wrong if you think—"

"Nope. I don't think so. I think you want ol' Andy real bad, so I don't figure five hundred clams is too much to ask. After all, those mags cost a bundle."

"Mags? What are you talking about?"

"Never mind. I've said more'n enough. You gonna buy or not?"

"Not," Margaret said emphatically before she replaced the receiver in its cradle.

She looked down at her trembling hands.

He knows where Andy is.

But revenge is no longer your business.

But he killed Angela.

Let it go.

You may never get another chance to find him.

Micah would never understand.

The phone rang again. "Hey, did you hang up on me?"

"What do chrome wheels have to do with finding Andy?"

"Nothin'. Whatcha talkin' 'bout?"

"Mags. You said those mags cost a bundle."

"Oh, that. Don't sweat it, lady. You just send me the money, and

114

I'll send you a copy of his address."

Margaret bit her lip. She had some money in savings, and Angela's life insurance would arrive soon. She could do this.

"You can call me back at 417—"

"No!" Her voice grew stronger. "No, and don't call here again."

She pressed the receiver in place and rose from her chair. Cat hit the floor with a thud, then raced to the kitchen. Margaret followed more slowly.

Mags. She knew Cliff said mags. What could he have meant, if not wheels? But that didn't make sense. As far as Margaret could remember, Andy had not chosen expensive accessories for his cars. Of course, she hadn't specifically asked anyone about his taste in cars.

She went to the refrigerator and pulled out the milk. She poured a glass for herself, then drained the near-empty container into Cat's dish.

It doesn't matter, she told herself. *I am NOT going to pursue Andy any longer.*

The next few weeks passed quickly, with Margaret sewing during the week, and on weekends she accompanied Micah to basketball games and church. Each Bible class helped her learn more about how God works in people's lives, and the discussions opened tiny windows of understanding of the degrees of trust various class members held. Some seemed to have developed a total acceptance of God's care and control; others, like herself, struggled with how to reach that goal; a few were bold enough to express a fear of letting go.

Micah patiently explained how they might as well relinquish their struggle to control all aspects of their lives, for even while they clutched around the edges of their problems, God had them sheltered in his hands, and already had the situation in control. If they would just do as much as they were able to cope, and turn the rest over to God, they would sleep better, and God would have more space to work his caring in their lives.

Micah said it was sort of like a small child refusing to trade a bare Popsicle stick for a new double Popsicle. He said if they would only let him, God would overwhelm them with blessings.

Margaret listened and fretted. She learned more every week, and her mind wrestled with each new tidbit. She made a concentrated effort to ban Andrew Bartimus from her mind, but each time she walked down the hall and saw Angela's pictures on the wall, her stomach lurched. She packed the photos away on a closet shelf.

Andrew didn't deserve to be allowed to walk the face of the earth free and unburdened by guilt. She felt he should be punished, but then she reminded herself that God could handle punishment without her help.

She would go a week or more, then open a drawer and find one of Angela's get well cards from when she first became ill. The hatred and anger roared over Margaret in a flash flood that encompassed her.

Margaret fought the urge to go to the bank and withdraw the five hundred dollars and drive to St. Robert. Better yet, she had Cliff's phone number. She could call and tell him to meet her half way, get the address, and be home in a little over two hours. Nobody but she and Cliff would know.

Instead, she went to the bank and switched her entire savings account to long-term certificates of deposit. If she cashed them in, she would have to pay a stiff penalty.

Now, the money won't be a temptation, she told herself only moments before Cat ran down the hall, made a leap onto the flowered chair, bounded to the end table, knocked over a figurine, then sprinted the length of the sofa.

"Bad Cat!" Margaret scolded, then picked up Cat and locked her in the bathroom. "A bit of contemplation will do you good," Margaret told the errant kitten.

Margaret returned to the end table and surveyed the damage. Grief engulfed her, and she sank onto the chair before great sobs wracked her whole body.

Only a month before her death, Angela had given Margaret the Hummel figure of a little girl and a goose.

"The girl is me and the goose is you," Angela had said. "You silly goose, you aren't supposed to cry all the time."

Memories flooded Margaret. She remembered bringing Angela home from the hospital and Henry carefully helping count their daughter's fingers and toes. Angela's first steps were for Henry, then Henry helped her learn to ride her bike, but Margaret was the one who walked her to school her first day. So many good times and so much promise, all wasted now. Margaret stared at the figurine. The little girl's arms were shattered and the goose's head was missing. Margaret had not been able to control her tears a few months ago, nor could she now.

She hated Andrew Bartimus.

One trip she was more than pleased to make was to the police station to identify Ed's attacker. It was the right man and Officer Smith told Margaret his name was Raymond Kensington. Apparently, there had been prior arrests resulting from the man's temper outbursts.

Micah asked permission to visit Raymond. "The Word may be able to break his chain of violence," he told Officer Smith.

"You can't be serious," Margaret said. "Just because Ed responded doesn't mean this man will. Ed didn't plan Cora's death—you two startled him into shooting. This guy sought Ed out and planned to attack him."

"I know, but the Word is a mighty sword," Micah said, as he walked toward the cell block. "I'll meet you at the hospital later."

As Margaret drove across town to meet Kathy, her mind raced. Did Micah think he could save the whole world? Some people just didn't want to be saved. Some didn't deserve to be. Like Raymond Kensington and Andrew Bartimus. She let the anger boil, then something began to niggle at her.

True, those two men were worthy of punishment, but what about herself? She had heard Mrs. Sanderson read that scripture in Bible class about not letting the sun go down on one's wrath. Did Margaret deserve to be saved any more than the two men she spent so much time condemning?

Margaret was reading her Bible quite a lot now, and she still watched *In Search of the Lord's Way* regularly. In the last program

she'd watched, Mack Lyon had said Jesus preached more about repentance than any other person had in the New Testament. Mr. Lyon
said Jesus commands everyone to repent. Margaret had flipped the
pages of her Bible to Acts 17:30-31 and II Peter 3:9, and on to Luke
13:3-5 right along with the preacher. She knew she could not legiti-
mately argue with Scripture, but she needed more time. Just as soon
as she found Andy and made him suffer, then she could consider
these things. Until then, she didn't want to think about them.

She was drawn to the TV program, and she knew Micah continued to pray for her. She also knew eventually she would have to let
her anger go. But not just yet.

She pushed that thought away, parked her car, and went inside
the hospital to find Kathy. She knocked gently on Ed's door, and at
Kathy's bidding, entered. Ed was awake, and a weak smile trans-
formed his face from a near-death mask to one of promise.

"Hello, lady."

"Well, hello, yourself. It's nice to hear your voice again."

The grin spread. "Yeah, to me, too." He grew serious. "Me and
Kathy have been talkin'. I'm gonna be down for quite a while. The
social worker here at the hospital is workin' with us to deal with the
bills here, but Kathy's gonna have to get a job."

"What about Desmond?" Margaret asked.

Kathy spoke. "The social worker says I'll qualify for free day care.
There's a licensed center just a few blocks from our apartment."

"That's wonderful," Margaret said. "Do you have any idea what
kind of job you want?"

"Not really. I took a few business classes in high school, but I'm
real rusty, not havin' a computer to practice on or anythin'."

"Have you been to the library?" Margaret asked. "I saw computers there. They might have some you could use to practice."

"No, but I imagine they're just full of library stuff. I need one with
a word processor."

Margaret nodded. "How soon are you going to look?"

"Today, I guess. I'll probably have to take a factory job 'til I can
practice my skills and get some decent clothes. Nothin' I own is fit to
wear in an office."

"Can you wait just a few more days? 'Til the end of the week?"

When Kathy stared at Margaret, she rushed on. "You're about the same size as my daughter, and she had lots of nice clothes. If it wouldn't offend you, I would love to see someone like you have them." Margaret hoped she wasn't being too impulsive.

Kathy stared. "Are you sure they would fit?"

"If not, I can alter them, since I made most of them in the first place."

Kathy rose to hug Margaret. "You're so nice. Thank you." Tears dampened the corners of Kathy's eyes, and she grabbed a tissue from Ed's nightstand.

Margaret continued. "Micah has a computer. He might let you practice on it a few days while I get the clothes in order."

"I forgot about that. Do you think he would mind?"

"I don't think so, but if he does, we'll find some other way to work it out."

Ed coughed and reached for his water. Margaret could tell he was still in a good bit of pain. Once he could speak, he said, "Why don't you two go see about those clothes, and let a poor guy get some rest?"

Kathy went to his side. "Are you sure you don't need me here?"

"I can reach the nurse's call button, and I'm really tired."

Kathy nodded.

Margaret admired Kathy's bravado, but she saw the quiver in the girl's lower lip. It had to be a frightening thing to suddenly be responsible for the support of her whole family, including what would undoubtedly be a horrendous hospital bill.

As they left the building, Margaret said, "I'll lead you to my house, but here's a map, just in case we get separated."

A half hour later, Margaret led Kathy to her sewing room in the basement. She pulled several large boxes from a closet. "Most of these are nearly new. I made them for Angela to wear to college, but she got sick and never wore a lot of them."

She slid the lid off the first box and lifted out a soft pastel-pink wool suit. "This must be the winter box. Let's try one of the others."

Kathy smoothed her hand over the wool and gasped. "This is

beautiful. I've never owned anything as nice as this."

Margaret smiled. "Wait 'til you see it all. Since I sew, we could afford some really nice outfits for much less than it would have cost to buy ready-made things."

She lifted a bright yellow shirtwaist dress from the second box and spread it across the arm of the sofa. Next she pulled out a lightweight poplin suit in beige, a lavender set, and a beautiful peach-colored outfit. Every one of them would compliment Kathy's rich brown features as well as they had Angela's fair ones.

"I think most of these will fit you," she said, holding a blouse up to Kathy. "There's a bathroom over there. Why don't you try on one or two things?"

Kathy picked up the peach outfit and left the room.

It pleased Margaret to see Kathy so excited over Angela's clothes. Each piece had been made with love, and Margaret couldn't stand the idea of just dumping them into a charity collection box. But to see someone actually wear Angela's things, and put them to good use, would be a real pleasure. Even beyond that, to know they could help Kathy get a much better job than she could be able to find otherwise filled Margaret with added joy.

Kathy returned, face beaming, but gripping the skirt with one hand. "It's a little big in the waist. Maybe if we set the button over?"

"Let me see," Margaret said. "I can alter it."

Kathy frowned. "Won't that be a lot of work?"

"Not too much." Margaret purposely made the alterations sound simple, though she knew they would take away even more time from the drapes waiting for her. She would just go to bed later and get up earlier for a while.

They spent a couple of hours pinning skirts and slacks to fit.

When they finished, Margaret said, "Now all you need are shoes and accessories. Let's go upstairs."

Kathy followed, her eyes full of puzzlement, but Margaret wanted to surprise her. She swallowed hard, then turned the knob and opened the door.

The Priscilla curtains hung crisp and full. The pink comforter on the bed lay smoothly, dripping its heavy lace edging over the darker pink skirting. The vanity sported a matching skirt with the same white lace border, top and bottom. Lace and ribbons bedecked the throw pillows that lay among the pink shams.

"What a lovely room," Kathy barely whispered. She stood at the door, obviously reluctant to enter.

"It's okay," Margaret said. "Angela's shoes are here in the closet."

She moved to the closet door and pulled it open. A full-length shoe bag hung on the inside, and each pocket was full.

"Here, try a pair," she told Kathy, as she handed over a pair of pink pumps.

Kathy looked for a place to sit, and Margaret said, "Sit on the bed."

Kathy did as Margaret indicated, then slipped off her tennis shoes.

"Wait," Margaret said when she saw Kathy's bobby socks.

She went to the dresser, opened a drawer, and rummaged around a bit. "Here." She handed Kathy a pair of nylon footlets.

Kathy slipped her foot into the pump, glanced up, and flashed Margaret a blinding smile.

"They fit! They really fit."

"Wonderful," Margaret said. "They're all yours. There are colors and styles to go with all the outfits downstairs."

"Oh, Margaret," Kathy began, then tears choked her. She stood and threw her arms around Margaret. "Thank you," she whispered. "I'm so scared, but maybe with your help, and Micah's, Ed and I may make it through this, too. Thank you."

Margaret patted Kathy and made little shushing sounds. "Of course, you're going to be fine."

But deep inside she wondered. How would they cope?

They carried the shoes to Kathy's car and loaded the tops and jackets, with Margaret promising to get the alterations done on the skirts within the next couple of days.

She couldn't quite bring herself to part with Angela's jewelry, both for sentimental reasons, and because she knew Kathy's taste would be different. The clothing Margaret had made was designed to be timeless and accept the latest trendy accents, so Kathy could make them uniquely her own. However, timeless equated to stark. Kathy needed those added touches, but money was a definite issue.

"Kathy, do you like to go to garage sales?"

"That's the only way Ed and I have survived. Almost all of Desmond's things came from sales all over the city."

"Good. There are a couple of community sales this weekend. Let's make a list of all the outfits that need accessories and go on a scavenger hunt Saturday morning."

"I don't know," Kathy began. "I'm not very good at that sort of thing. I always look like the trash truck turned over on me."

Margaret laughed. "No, you don't, but I'll help you. Let's grab a sandwich and a glass of milk, then we'll go back down and make our list."

The church drapes would just have to wait.

Chapter Seventeen

On Saturday, Kathy called Margaret. "I'm not going to be able to get away. I can't find anyone to keep Desmond, and even if I could, I can't afford to pay anyone."

"Do you have a stroller?"

"Yes. It's old, but we still use it."

"Then bring it and the baby, and we'll shop 'til he gets tired, and we'll quit."

"Are you sure you don't mind?"

"Of course not. The weather's nice, and we'll be walking from house to house anyway."

"I'll be there in about twenty minutes."

Margaret pushed Cat off her lap and went to tie a scarf around her unruly hair. For some reason, a comb seemed powerless to tame it this morning. She checked her purse to be sure she had the list of outfits they needed to accessorize, as well as scraps of fabric she'd taken time to locate.

A few minutes later, she heard a car pull into her driveway and hurried to meet Kathy. They had already decided Kathy would drive, so they wouldn't have to move Desmond's car seat from one vehicle to another.

Margaret slid into the front seat beside Kathy, then twisted to speak to Desmond. "Hi, pumpkin. How are you this morning?"

Desmond squealed and kicked in delight.

"I think he recognizes me!"

"'Course he does. You been with him 'most as much as I have lately," Kathy said, "an' he likes you."

Margaret smiled, but her heart ached. Desmond was probably as close as she would ever come to having a grandchild. She loved this baby as much as any grandmother ever could, but he didn't fill that hole in her heart where Angela's children would have fit. When people talked about dealing with grief by becoming involved with others' needs, they didn't understand that you could fill your hours, and you could love other people with an unbelievable intensity; but no matter how hard you worked, it didn't fill the void left by the loss of a loved one.

As Kathy drove toward the Meadowbrook North community, Margaret reflected that her ongoing sense of loss gave a new perspective to her understanding of the parable of the lost sheep.

Of course, the Good Shepherd would leave the ninety-nine and go looking for the lost lamb, if he missed that one as much as Margaret missed Angela. She decided not to think about it any more this morning. This was supposed to be an enjoyable outing.

"Oh, look," Kathy exclaimed when they reached an entryway into the subdivision. "I don't know where I'll be able to park."

Cars lined both sides of the street, leaving a single lane for traffic .

"Go down a couple of blocks. We can walk back," Margaret said. She laughed when she saw people rushing from house to house, arms and shopping bags already brimming with their bargain buys. Each garage spewed a conglomerate of unneeded items on display for sale. Some of the driveways were lined on both sides by furniture, bicycles, and boxes of small items and books. Improvised tables sagged under the loads of no-longer-cherished treasures.

Kathy advanced slowly to avoid hitting the people who darted from one side of the street to the other in a race to find the best bargains.

"There's a parking spot," Margaret said when an old beat-up pickup truck pulled out to move farther down the street. Kathy nosed in and parked. She went to the back of the van to get the stroller while Margaret unbuckled Desmond from the car seat. When she lifted the wiry little boy, he laughed and patted her face and wriggled.

"Come on, big guy. Let's go join the throngs." She laughed at his excitement.

"He loves to ride," Kathy said. She unfolded the compact umbrella stroller, and Margaret buckled Desmond in.

The two women spent the next two hours walking from garage to garage, examining vast arrays of every sort of merchandise anyone could imagine. It was like a treasure hunt through everything from trash to triumphs—white elephants to white diamonds—all there for a price.

Kathy stood before a table fitted with knick-knacks, kitchenwares, and a display of costume jewelry. She lifted a necklace of heavy gold-colored links that Margaret knew would be perfect on the olive green sheath at home.

"There's no price on it," Kathy said.

Margaret located the owner and asked, "How much is the jewelry?"

The woman eyed Margaret's well-fitted gray slacks and costly pink sweater. "Five dollars."

"I don't think so," Margaret told Kathy. "We'll find something else."

They started to move away, but the woman called after them. "Five dollars for the whole box full of stuff."

Kathy stopped and grinned. "What do you think?"

Margaret turned and looked. There were three gold chains, the linked piece Kathy liked so well, a frivolous necklace of hand-carved wooden animals and beads, three chunky gold bracelets, and several pairs of earrings in golds and bright colored "stones."

"Sold," Margaret said before she scooped up as much as she could hold and watched Kathy gather up the rest.

A few houses farther along, Margaret bought Desmond a fuzzy black stuffed puppy with a bright red bow around its neck.

"You shouldn't spoil him like that," Kathy said.

Margaret shrugged and grinned. "It's only a quarter, and he loves it. Look at him."

Kathy laughed. "He does, doesn't he?"

By the time they had worked through the whole neighborhood, Kathy had jewelry, scarves, and belts to match every outfit on their list. Margaret added a dressy winter coat, a set of hot curlers to help keep Kathy's hair looking nice, and a bag full of toys for Desmond.

Kathy had spent seven dollars and fifty cents. Margaret spent six dollars. They dumped their bags and the stroller into the back of the van and slid a now cranky Desmond into his car seat.

"I'll sit in back and give him a bottle while you drive," Margaret said.

"Are you sure you don't mind? I could feed him, and we could go after that."

"No. Let's get on over to Claymont. I would still like to find some small flower pots for the violets I have sprouted all over my kitchen."

"I forgot about those," Kathy said. "I've been too excited over all my stuff to think about what you needed."

"No problem," Margaret said. "I was looking but didn't find anything here." Kathy drove, and Desmond gulped, while Margaret slipped off her shoes and wriggled her cramped toes.

At Claymont, the crowds had thinned, so parking was easier. Once again, the women pushed a contented Desmond from garage to garage, but by now, there were few choice items left. They crossed the street and headed back toward the car when Margaret spotted a couple of large boxes in front of the next garage. When she pushed Desmond close, she saw piles of small clay pots, and even saucers to go with them. A black-marker scrawl said "five cents."

She pushed Desmond over to Kathy. "If you'll go get the van, I'll watch Desmond and pay for all these. I don't think we can carry them that far."

Kathy nodded and sprinted off toward the van.

Margaret turned to the man at the cash box. "Do you know how many pots are in there?"

"Naw, probably close to seventy-five, and they's saucers to all of 'em, too."

"I want them all, so I guess I need to set them out and count them." She squatted and reached inside the box.

"No need, 'less you really want to. I'll take three-fifty fer the whole mess."

Margaret did a quick calculation. "Are you sure? That's less than half the price marked on the box."

"Naw, it ain't. It's five cents a set. You want 'em, you got 'em. I just want 'em outta here."

"Sold." Margaret reached into her purse and counted out the money. A little spray paint, a few pieces of ribbon around the rims, and these would be real room brighteners for Micah's nursing-home friends. It felt wonderful to be able to do something nice for someone else—even people she didn't know.

When they arrived at Kathy's house, Desmond's head drooped to one side in a sound sleep.

"Give me the keys," Margaret said, "and I'll bring your stuff. You go ahead and take the baby in to bed."

"Thanks." Kathy lifted Desmond from his seat without seeming to disturb him a bit.

Margaret gathered as much as she could carry from the back of the van and followed Kathy. When she reached the house, she looked up in surprise at Micah holding the door open.

"Hello. I didn't expect to see you here," she said.

"I came by to tell Kathy about Ed's morale."

"And?"

"Not as good as I hoped, but better than I expected," Micah said in soft tones.

"I know. It's slow going." She smiled and extended the bags she held. "But we have Kathy all set to go out and knock those personnel managers' socks off."

Kathy joined them. "Got it all?"

"Not yet. I've been too busy talking to Micah."

"I'll go," the younger woman said.

Micah took the opportunity of her absence to say, "It's really nice of you to help her like this. It could make all the difference in the world in the kind of job she finds."

Margaret met Micah's searching gaze and felt a blush flood her face. The sensation flustered her even more. It was ridiculous for a woman her age to feel the emotions Micah evoked in her, and it was even more ludicrous for her to blush. Butterflies and blushing were for young women, for heaven's sake!

"I'm glad I can help," she stammered, "but it remains to be seen if it helps that much."

"It will," Micah said, and Margaret's heart raced when Micah squeezed her elbow.

Kathy pushed through the door with her sack full of goodies. She dumped the bag on the sofa and exclaimed, "I'm rich, and now I'll be beautiful."

Margaret was delighted when Micah said, "You always were beautiful. That stuff is just the setting for the real jewel."

Kathy cuffed his sleeve, "Stop that. You're embarrassing me."

Micah turned to Margaret. "Could I drive you home, since Desmond's asleep? It would be a shame for Kathy to have to drag him out of bed."

"I'd appreciate it," she said, "but I have a couple of boxes of flower pots we'll have to move from her van to your car."

"I can handle that," Micah said. "Are those by any chance going to be used for new violet plants?"

"But, of course."

At Margaret's house, she opened the garage door and told Micah to set her boxes on the workbench.

"Come on in, and I'll fix us a sandwich," she said. "It's already lunchtime."

Micah dusted his hands. "Don't mind if I do."

Margaret pulled a package of pressed ham, and one of sliced cheese, and a jar of sweet pickles from the refrigerator. "I have sodas, coffee, tea, or milk. What's your pleasure?"

"Milk sounds nice."

Margaret went to the cupboard and got plates and glasses.

"Micah," she asked, "why did God allow that man to ruin Ed's and Kathy's lives like that?"

She hadn't meant to ask, but ever since Ed had crumpled at her feet, she couldn't get the question out of her mind—or the anger out of her heart.

Micah hesitated a moment, and she knew he was searching for the right words. But when he spoke, it was in a tone of confidence.

"I can't give you an exact, specific reason, but I can tell you with all assurance that something good will come out of this. It may not always seem good for Kathy and Ed, but someone will be blessed by all this."

"How can you say that? Ed's crippled for life. Kathy's doomed to be the family's support. She'll never be able to stay home and mother Desmond. It just isn't fair."

"Margaret, God never promised we would think everything he allows is fair. He also never promised to exempt us from Satan and his influences. What God did promise was that all things would work together for good for his children. Even the bad things."

"How could Ed's injury ever turn out for good? I just don't see it."

Micah reached over and patted her hand. "If it's any comfort to you, right now I don't either. But God promised, and I believe his promises." The soft smile reached his eyes, and Margaret swallowed under his scrutiny.

He continued. "We may never in this lifetime know why, but then again, given time we might. When Ed shot Cora, it made no sense at all to me, but through her death, Ed and Kathy were converted, and it has opened a door to work with LaMont and his friends. Cora would gladly have died twice to see that kind of success."

"But the man who shot Ed won't even see you. You're not likely to convert him."

"Probably not, but that may not be God's purpose this time. He may be using this to draw Ed and Kathy closer to him, or it may be to help you, or someone like you, understand, or it could be for some reason we will never see or know. The only thing absolutely certain is that it will work out for the best. God has never broken a promise in all of recorded history."

Margaret stared at her hands and wished there was some way she could believe as strongly as Micah did, but right now she just couldn't.

"I guess I just don't have your faith," she said. "I wish I did, but the raw truth is, I don't."

"If you really want to strengthen your faith, there's a guaranteed formula to do it."

Margaret glanced up from the sandwich she sliced.

"Faith cometh by hearing, and hearing by the word of God," Micah quoted. "All you have to do is read and listen to God's word with an open mind, and there's no way you can come away not believing his promises."

"Do you really think so?"

"I know so. You start reading your Bible every day, and come to Bible classes and church services to hear the discussions, and I guarantee your faith will grow by leaps and bounds, to borrow a cliche."

Margaret shrugged. "Maybe."

Micah clasped her hand and gave it a firm squeeze. "God promised it would turn out well. Grow your faith, and watch those two young people develop their strength."

Margaret shook her head in frustration. "I'm not so sure."

"Just let the Word work its stuff, and you'll see. In the meantime, are you too tired to take in another basketball game? Tonight's the last championship game. The Hawks are up to win." Micah's eyes glowed in pleasure, and his mouth quirked in a lopsided grin.

It saddened her to think Ed wouldn't be able to see the game, but when Margaret glanced up at Micah's one lifted eyebrow, she laughed. "How could I miss something that important?"

Chapter Eighteen

When they arrived, the gym was less than full, but the few people who had come early milled about talking in excited bursts and much animation. The very air seemed electric.

Micah led Margaret to a seat directly behind the Hawks' bench. He looked at her sheepishly. "I'll be busy with the guys, and I tend to get carried away, especially when we're this close to the championship."

Margaret waved a hand. "I wouldn't have it any other way. Lukewarm basketball fans aren't any more profitable than lukewarm Christians."

Micah's grin spread. "You've been reading your Bible."

"Yes, but don't press your luck. The jury's still out."

Micah nodded, but his eyes twinkled when he said, "The Lord always wins." He glanced toward the court. "I'm sorry, but I need to talk to the boys. I hope you enjoy the game, and I promise I'll make up for neglecting you."

Margaret shook her head. "Don't worry about me, Micah. I'll be fine, and you have a responsibility to those boys. Go do your job, and see that they win!"

"Will do," Micah said before he turned and sprinted toward the dressing room.

When the team appeared for warm ups, Margaret grinned and cheered along with the other people who were rapidly filling the bleachers.

Micah moved from the edge of the court to the coach's bench just as one of the referees blew his whistle for the game to begin. He cheered, leaned forward and watched, then bolted upright and shouted instructions to the players on the court. Margaret was not knowledgeable enough to appreciate the nuances of the game, but she did enjoy watching Micah and the other fans. By their reactions, she could tell when the game was going well, or when a player did less than his best.

At two minutes before half-time, the score was an even thirty-six to thirty-six. Margaret grew as excited as the people around her. By this time, Micah alternated between perching on the bench and pacing the edge of the playing floor.

"Do you see how those guys are playing? We have to pump it up in this last half. Our boys are counting on going to state."

The crowd roared, and both teams raced from one end of the court to the other and back, so fast that the only sense Margaret had of what had transpired was through the scoreboard. When the half-time whistle blew, the score was forty to forty.

Margaret smiled when Micah sprinted across the gym floor. *Not bad for an old guy,* she thought. Pride swelled her breast when she watched Micah speak and touch the players. It would be impossible for anyone to miss the respect each held for the other. The whole team worked as a well-conducted symphony, never missing a beat. Micah had done that, and his efforts were paying off.

Margaret glanced around, spotted a soft-drink vendor, and decided she was thirsty. By the time she worked her way back to her seat, Micah had returned to the floor. He nodded and gave her a quick thumbs up.

"How's the team holding up?" she called out.

Micah jogged over. "They're really pumped. Our defense seems to have an edge. If we can utilize that, we should be able to take this game to the bank!"

Margaret giggled. "Did you realize you slip into the kids' cliched jargon when you get excited?"

Micah blinked. "I do?"

They both laughed, before Micah moved back to the court. Margaret felt wonderful. It was so nice to share times like this with Micah.

The second half of the game flew by, and Margaret blinked when the final whistle blew. The scoreboard read 96-97, Hawks! The crowd roared. Micah was caught up in hugs and backslaps in the middle of the team members as they swept into the dressing rooms.

After several minutes, Micah returned to Margaret's side. "We're going to take LaMont home, if that's okay with you?"

"That's fine," she agreed.

"We'll have to wait a bit, but it shouldn't be too long."

Margaret sat back on the bleacher and watched the people leave the gymnasium. Those on the side she occupied laughed and talked in animated voices, and joked among themselves. Many of those on the opposite side hugged one another, offered tissues to blot escaped tears, and left the building in a subdued mood. Margaret's heart ached for those who lost, for they fought a valiant battle right to the end, but she couldn't help being joyous for LaMont and his friends. Scholarships had hung in the balance, and now theirs were assured.

Margaret looked up and saw LaMont bound around the perimeter of the gym, his grin as hugely out of proportion as his feet and hands. "Man, oh man, we're hot!"

Margaret thrust her right fist into the air. "On to state!"

LaMont spewed exuberance for his teammates, Micah, and the whole basketball association, until Margaret marveled that his lips didn't grow numb from the vibration.

She laughed. "LaMont, I shudder to think how you would have acted if you had lost."

"But we didn't!" he shouted. "We didn't!"

She breathed a silent prayer. "Thank you, God, for this victory."

"The other guys will be here in a couple o' seconds. Where're we gonna eat? I'm starved."

Margaret groaned. "I forgot you guys wait until after the game to eat. It seems as though I'm always eating with Micah!"

"Sounds right to me," LaMont said. "Let's go have pizza, okay?"

"Ummm," Micah said.

Yin Ling and Hector jogged over and said in unison, "Let's eat!"

"Come on," Micah said, and he led Margaret to the exit. The boys chatted, joked, and jostled one another along in excitement over their win.

When they reached the parking lot, a couple of men were entering a van next to Micah's car. Margaret stood back to allow them room, but in his exuberance Hector bumped into her back. It startled her, and she stumbled forward, into the man.

"Oh, I'm sorry," she said to the man at the same time Hector grabbed her arm to keep her from completely losing her balance.

"Hey, I'm sorry," Hector rushed to say, open terror etched on his face.

Margaret remembered Ed's encounter, as she was sure Hector did.

"Watch it," the man snarled in almost the same instant. "You inner-city kids all think it's cool to party and abuse other people, but I won't put up with it. Back off!"

Margaret gasped.

"Look, man, we just won the game inside," Yin Ling said. "We may be a little rowdy, but we're not high. My friend here said he was sorry, and he meant it."

Margaret held her breath. Would this man react as Raymond Kinsington had in that earlier, almost identical, encounter only a few weeks ago?

Oh, God, don't let this get out of hand, she prayed. *Not again.*

The man eyed Yin Ling, then snapped, "Just let us outta here."

Yin Ling pulled at Margaret's arm to back her from between the vehicles. Nobody said a word, but Margaret noticed Micah had somehow moved between her and the insolent man. Realization of what he had done, and his undeniable reason overwhelmed her. Tears ran down her cheeks unchecked until well after the van's taillights disappeared down the street.

"Let's get out of here," Hector said. He jerked the front car door open for Margaret, then the rear one for LaMont and himself. Micah and Yin Ling climbed in from the other side.

Micah started the engine and pulled out of the lot. Nobody spoke. It was as though some giant hand had reached down and smacked the laughter and joy from the air.

The heaviness nearly smothered Margaret. All she could think was, *Thank you, God, for your protection tonight.*

Later that night, when she was alone, she marveled at how naturally that prayer came to her, and how right it had seemed.

Maybe God did have a place in her life.

The day Ed came home from the hospital called for a celebration. Micah and the boys had built a ramp to the house to accommodate Ed's wheelchair, and Margaret and Kathy tied bright-colored balloons and crepe-paper streamers on the porch rails. A cake and punch bowl sat on the kitchen table atop a white lace tablecloth. Red and blue napkins lay in a neat row next to the bright-yellow forks. Micah brought folding chairs, but this would be a come-and-go affair. No way could Kathy's home hold all at one time the two to three hundred people they expected.

Desmond stood balanced in a walker and laughed at Margaret when she pulled her hands from over her face and said, "Boo!" They repeated the game several times, until Margaret heard Micah's car in the drive.

She picked up Desmond and went to the window to watch as Kathy and Micah positioned the wheelchair and helped Ed out of the car. Someone else drove up to the curb and dropped off LaMont, Hector, and Yin Ling.

LaMont ran to help Ed, while the other two boys hurried to open the door. Margaret brushed the tears from the corners of her eyes and blew her nose. These were tears of joy, but she didn't want them on display for the whole world to see. It seemed her whole emotional repertoire had tilted out of control lately. Joy brought tears, being with Micah evoked feelings she thought were long ago dead, and fear evoked prayers. Even her anger seemed to be dissipating. She hardly knew her own inner self anymore. She smiled when Hector and Yin Ling did a vocal rendition of a royal trumpet prelude, and Kathy pushed Ed through the door.

"There's my guy!" Ed said when he spotted Desmond. He reached out for the baby, and Margaret held him down for his father.

"Boy, you've grown while I was gone!" Ed said. He hugged Desmond until the baby began to fuss and squirm. Ed laughed and loosened his hold. "Okay. I'll lighten up. How's that?" he asked when he set Desmond on his knees and just looked at him.

"Sorry I can't bounce you," he said lightly.

The room grew silent, and Margaret saw LaMont and his friends glance at the floor in embarrassed frustration. She squatted beside Ed. "But you can play peek-a-boo. He likes that. I'll hold him for you."

She braced Desmond on his father's lap and felt a surge of joy when Ed uncovered his face and said, "Boo!"

The whole room burst into laughter when Desmond giggled at his daddy's antics.

The doorbell rang, and Kathy told Ed, "I hope you don't mind, but we invited the people from church to come by and have refreshments to welcome you home. Everyone's been so good to us."

Ed smiled. "It'll be good to see them all."

Margaret handed Desmond to Hector and went to put the ice ring in the punch bowl. In only a few minutes, the small house was overflowing, and people hugged and talked, and wished Ed and Kathy well.

Margaret served the cake and punch and observed many of the people place envelopes on the table. Nobody mentioned a card. Each person just quietly laid one down and walked away.

Bruce Jacobson came and spoke to Margaret, got a cup of punch, then turned to Ed. "Well, young man, you look a lot better than you did the last time I saw you."

"I feel a lot better, too," Ed said.

"I tried to come to see you at the hospital, but they wouldn't let me in while you were in ICU, and after you were moved to a private room, you were in physical therapy every time I showed up."

"They did keep me pretty busy most of the time."

Bruce grew more serious. "Have the doctors said anything about any job training yet?"

"Not a lot. They mentioned a sheltered workshop downtown, but I'll have to go through a bunch of screening tests first, and I don't know how I'd manage transportation, especially with Kathy working her job."

"Yeah! I heard about the position she got at that investment company. Congratulations! That was a real stroke of luck. Nice job, I hear."

Ed shook his head. "Not luck. Some people helped her get ready for the interview, but God got her the job. God's been here through this whole thing."

Bruce nodded. "You're right, of course, and I'm glad to see you recognize it. When does she start?"

"Monday, and she's kinda nervous about it."

"She'll do just fine. Kathy's a bright lady. She'll have that new boss so organized, he'll be able to do twice the work he's ever done before."

Kathy walked up to stand beside Ed. "I hope so. They'll be paying me enough to need to triple their production, not to mention the extra benefits I'll get after a three month probationary period." Kathy's eyes gleamed with pride.

"Good for you," Bruce said. "It's about time things took an upturn."

In a sudden shift, he asked, "Ed, have you ever done anything with computers?"

"No. I told you a long time ago, I don't even know how to turn one on. Why?"

Bruce shook his head. "Oh, I was just thinking, but I guess it was a bad idea."

He set his glass on the table and patted Ed on the shoulder. "Good to see you home, man. I gotta run, but we'll see you back in church soon."

"Sure thing," Ed said.

A couple of hours later, everyone was gone except Margaret and Micah. Margaret wrapped the remaining cake in foil and poured the small amount of leftover punch into a pitcher to be refrigerated.

"Kathy, there are bunches of cards here you and Ed might like to read," she said. Kathy took the envelopes and went to sit beside Ed's chair. Ed reached out and took the top envelope and tore it open. When he lifted the card out, a fifty dollar bill fluttered into his lap.

"What . . . ?" he asked, then shook his head. "We can't accept this."

Micah came over and looked solemnly at Ed. "Yes, you can. These people wanted to help you and Kathy all along, but especially now, in your time of special need. Many can't give time, but they can give money—money you need, right now. This, too, is a lesson from God. Sometimes it takes a much stronger Christian to accept help than it does to refuse it.

"Even the apostle Paul was given monetary help at times, and he used it to glorify God. In turn, it blessed many other people's lives. Your challenge is not to refuse this help, but to make it bless not only you, but others as well."

Ed stared at Micah a long moment, so long Margaret feared he would still refuse, but finally, he swallowed and nodded slowly. "I'll do my best," he promised.

Ed and Kathy opened the remaining cards, and each one held a folded bill or a check. When they finished, Margaret watched Kathy count up almost five thousand dollars. Kathy cried openly, and even Ed wiped his nose on his sleeve. "Why're they so good to us?" he asked.

"Because you're family," Micah said, "and families take care of one another." He hugged both Ed and Kathy.

"I have one more surprise for you. Bruce had me walk him out, and he said his company is updating their computers. He asked me if I thought Ed might like to have one of the old ones to keep him from being so bored. I guess Bruce is quite a computer-game enthusiast, and his personal unit has a bunch of games already installed. It should be here tomorrow, unless I call him and tell him not to send it."

Ed's brows lifted before his frown settled. "I don't know nothin' 'bout computers. I'd probably break it."

Micah laughed. "It's called crash, but nearly every kid in the country has mastered computer games, and your brain's still intact. You should be able to get the hang of it soon enough."

"I don't know. I hate for Bruce to be out so much expense."

"You stop that, Ed Johnson. Bruce wants to help you, and the days can get awfully long with nothing to do. Trashy day-time TV and four walls looking at you aren't too entertaining. Kathy and Desmond will be gone, you know."

Ed nodded. "I know. Every day at the hospital got to be an eternity long, and I never want to see another day-time TV show."

Kathy winked at Micah, and Margaret asked, "So where do you want us to clear a space to set it up?"

Ed and Kathy glanced around. Ed spoke first. "In our bedroom, I guess."

Kathy shook her head. "I don't think so. There's not much light, and you can't see outside. How about over by the front window, here in the living room?"

Margaret smiled. In a more modern, more expensive house, this would be called the "great room," but here, in this modest little home, it was simply the living room. Ed surveyed the area Kathy indicated. "Ain't room. Over here by the center wall would be better."

Kathy shook her head. "No, we can move that chair over here. You need to be able to see outside, if you want to."

"I like that chair right there," Ed said.

Kathy cuffed his sleeve lightly. "Would you stop? I'm tryin' to give ya an office with a window like the rich folks."

Micah broke in. "And that's rather appropriate, don't you think? Look at how rich the two of you are. You have a nice home, a beautiful baby, and lots of friends who love you."

"And," Kathy added, "tomorrow, an office by the window!"

Ed laughed. "Okay, so move the chair."

Once that was done, Ed looked at Micah. "If I'm gonna be a man of leisure from now on, who you gonna get to do all that stuff up at the church building?"

Micah shook his finger back and forth. "I already have that under control. LaMont asked for your job while you were in the hospital—just to be sure nobody else took it before you came back. He's so good at it, we're planning on keeping him."

"You firing me?" Ed joked.

"Nope. We're holding the space for you 'til you're ready to come back. We'll kick LaMont into some other worthwhile project when you're ready. Your job, right now, is to get to feeling better and get back up to that building."

Ed's smile was weak. "That may take some time."

"Yes," Kathy agreed, "and you've had a full day. It's time for you to rest."

"Yes, Mama," Ed said in a teasing tone.

But Margaret saw the lines of weariness around his eyes. "I think it's time for you to drive me home, Micah."

"Agreed," he said, and took her arm. "You two take care, and we'll see you in a few days."

Chapter Nineteen

*O*n Monday, Kathy went to her job at the investment company, and Ed was to spend his first day at home alone. Margaret worked to finish the draperies for the church before the coming weekend. She wondered how Ed was doing. Her fingers and her mind worked in swift unison. One more hem and she would be ready to deliver everything, just in time for the planned homecoming service.

Micah was expecting former members to return from all over the United States. He'd said one family was even driving back from Costa Rica for this day.

Margaret wondered what Micah's sermon topic would be. She decided she would be there to hear it, but today she needed to work.

By late afternoon, she had finished the last stitches; then she called Micah. "If I come up now, will LaMont be there to help me hang the rest of the new drapes?"

"Certainly. Come on up," Micah said. "We'll be glad to see you."

Margaret smiled at the warmth in Micah's voice, which in turn raised her temperature. *Careful, girl,* she told herself as she drove to the church. *Micah's a very nice man, but he's a preacher, and you're not even a member of the church. Just get your head on straight, and stop this teenage panting.*

She wheeled into the parking lot and parked. Before she could step out and open the trunk, LaMont sprinted up. "I can carry those," he said.

"Thanks. They're a handful."

Micah held the heavy double doors and told them to go directly into the auditorium.

LaMont set the box down next to the pulpit and went to get the ladder.

"This is wonderful," Micah said. "I was afraid you might not be able to finish before this weekend. You've spent a lot of time with

Kathy and Ed, and it would have been understandable if you hadn't, but this is so nice."

"I haven't done all that much for those kids, and I just worked a few evenings to catch up. Now, I'm all done—if these things hang straight."

"They will. You do very good work. In fact, I've already been asked for your phone number by three women here in the congregation."

"That's good. I had begun to wonder if there was work after the church job."

Her stomach did funny things, and her pulse raced when Micah laughed with her.

"I'm sure you'll be even busier than you want to be."

"Hey, you two, how about a hand here?" LaMont called.

Margaret reluctantly broke her gaze away from Micah and walked over to slip the hooks into the drapery header and hoist each piece up to LaMont. Micah steadied the ladder as LaMont stretched to place each panel correctly.

When he finished and climbed down, they all three stepped back and surveyed the finished result.

"Wow!" LaMont said. "That's awesome. Look at how the spotlights make those threads shimmer."

Micah burst out laughing and turned to Margaret. "I think your efforts are a success. Who else in the entire world could get a teenage boy excited over drapes?"

Margaret looked over at the sheepish LaMont and burst into laughter when he shrugged.

"Well, they do look awesome," he defended himself.

Micah and Margaret laughed even harder.

"You two are nuts," LaMont said. "I'm gonna put this ladder back where it belongs!" He picked it up and scurried away.

Micah turned to Margaret. "So, will you be here Sunday?"

"I suppose so," Margaret said. "I'll have to see this homecoming you've planned for so long."

"Good! I think you'll find it enlightening."

On Sunday morning, Margaret thought "enlightening" was hardly the word. "Overwhelming" was more like it. People overflowed out of the pews and into folding chairs up the outer aisles, and even between the front row of pews and the pulpit. Margaret was thankful she'd arrived early enough to get a center-aisle seat. She could see and hear Micah quite well from where she sat.

Once Micah got into his sermon, she wasn't so comfortable. He had chosen the topic of "Homecoming to God." He spoke of how enjoyable it was to have old friends and family to worship with them this morning. He expressed a sense of sadness over those who were unable to come, and an even greater grief over those who had left the faith over time.

Margaret had expected something similar, but then he turned the emphasis to the final homecoming with God, and how joyous God would be to receive the faithful, and the great grief he would feel for those who had never become members of his family.

Micah talked about the terrible loss of inheritance those unbelievers would experience: "God has a mansion sitting on a street of gold, and a glorious crown for the faithful. He offers forgiveness of sin and everlasting joy for those who believe and come to him. He requires us to forgive and to repent, but we can become heirs to his throne."

Margaret squirmed. She twisted the kerchief in her hand. She smoothed her skirt. She thumbed through her Bible. But she listened all the while Micah talked.

By the time Micah said, "If you're not a child of God, won't you come forward now while we stand and sing?" Margaret was broken. She stepped into the aisle, and with tears streaming freely down her face, she went to claim God's forgiveness in baptism.

Micah grasped her hands and his look of compassion nearly overwhelmed Margaret. She could imagine Jesus greeting her with that same tenderness and concern.

When Micah asked, "Margaret, do you believe Jesus is the Christ, the Son of God?" her sincere affirmation startled her. She hadn't thought she would be capable of speech for the lump that clogged her throat.

When she stepped into the baptistry, and Micah said the age-old words, "I now baptize you in the name of the Father, the Son, and the Holy Spirit," she automatically held her breath. It was not only to prevent the water from entering her lungs as she was submerged, but more than that, it was her natural response to the awe of dying to her old sins and having them washed away, so she could be once again pure before God. It had been a very long time since she'd felt truly spotless.

Micah lifted her back to her feet, and oblivious to what it would do to his shirt, he gripped Margaret in a fierce hug and whispered, "Welcome home, Margaret. The angels are rejoicing with us today."

Margaret swept the water from her face, uncaring that it mixed with her tears of joy. Now her task was to keep herself as pure as God wanted her to be.

All seemed right with Margaret's world at last. At least it seemed so until the day Kathy called, crying.

"Margaret, do you have a few minutes to talk if I come by in about half an hour?"

"Of course I do, Kathy." Margaret glanced at her watch. One-fifteen. Kathy should be at work.

"What's wrong, Kathy? Is Ed okay?"

"Yes—yes, he's fine, but—oh, I can't explain on the phone. I'm on my way over."

The phone clicked, and Margaret stared at the instrument in her hand as though it could spontaneously impart the knowledge she sought. Finally, she replaced the receiver in its cradle and went to the kitchen to turn on the teakettle. A nice cup of tea always seemed to calm the nerves, or at least gave the distraught something to do with their hands.

Cat galloped into the kitchen and skidded into Margaret's legs, then began an insistent mewing.

"You think every time I come into the kitchen you get something?" Margaret nudged Cat with her foot. "Scoot."

What could have Kathy so upset at this time of day, especially if it wasn't a problem with Ed? Could the baby be sick? Surely not, or Kathy would have said something.

Cat meowed again.

"Okay!" Margaret poured a small portion of cat chow into Cat's bowl.

She pulled out a pretty pressed-glass plate and arranged some chocolate-chip cookies on it. Why was Kathy crying? Margaret was sure she'd heard Kathy sniff, and the break in her voice was unmistakable. And why would Kathy leave her office in the middle of the day?

Margaret slipped into prayer. "Lord, let me help her, whatever the problem is. We both know you're the answer to every trouble we face."

The doorbell rang, and Margaret rushed to let Kathy in. One look at the young woman, and Margaret's worst fear was realized. Kathy's face was streaked with tears, her makeup either smeared or, in places, totally wiped away.

She threw herself into the arms Margaret held open. Margaret uttered soothing words, smoothed Kathy's wooly hair, and hugged her tightly, while the young woman sobbed.

After several minutes, Kathy pulled away. "I'm sorry. I just didn't know where else to go, or what to do." Tears flowed again, and she tried to find a dry spot on her crumpled tissue to blow her nose.

"Come on." Margaret pulled Kathy toward the kitchen. She grabbed a box of tissues from the hall table and handed Kathy one. Kathy blew her nose, and Margaret led her to a chair and sat her at the table, then sat opposite her.

"Now, tell me what this is all about."

Kathy struggled for composure and blotted her eyes a few seconds before she could speak. "Oh, Margaret," she wailed. "I lost my job! How can I go home and tell Ed? What will we do?"

The tissue lay in shreds on the table and Kathy pulled another from the box.

"Oh, honey, how awful for you. What happened?" Margaret reached out and took Kathy's hands in her own in an effort to impart comfort through touch.

"That's what's so bad. I don't know what happened. I went in this morning, and everything was normal."

Kathy hiccoughed, and she and Margaret both laughed nervously.

Kathy continued. "I made some calls for my boss, and I did some research in the files he'd asked for. When I gave the information to him, he seemed really pleased. In fact, he told me I'd done a great job."

"So what happened?" Margaret asked when Kathy paused and hiccoughed again.

"Well, I went to lunch with a couple of the girls, and when we came back, our pay checks had arrived. My boss asked me to come into his office when he gave me mine. I did, and he hemmed and hawed, but finally he mumbled something about things being slow, and he told me the check was for my regular pay and two weeks' severance pay. He said I could go home right then."

"Oh, Kathy, I'm so sorry. Did he say anything about you being able to go back later?"

"No. I asked him, and he said the cutbacks will be permanent." She hiccoughed again. "He even had the nerve to mumble something about how I might look back and thank him for this some day!"

Of all the insensitive things for someone to say! Margaret felt her rage boiling up. Why had God allowed this to happen to Kathy? Didn't he understand how desperately Kathy needed that job? Where was the justice in all this? Where was the kind, loving, in-control God Micah talked about? All things work together for good? Right! Kathy, the only wage-earner in her family, landed a really good job, then had it snatched away, and all that was for her good? Margaret didn't see how. She wanted to—but she just could not see how this could be a good thing.

Kathy needed her salary. Just by looking at her, Margaret could see how emotionally destructive this had been to Kathy's self-esteem. Margaret wanted to scream, "Where are you, God?"

Instead, she poured herself and Kathy a cup of tea. "Kathy, it'll work out. You'll be okay." She, like Kathy, wasn't sure what she said was true, but she knew Kathy needed to hear it right now, true or not.

She rushed on. "You have two weeks' severance pay. That gives you two weeks to find another job. You're in no shape this afternoon, but tomorrow morning you get the newspaper and bounce right back out there looking again."

"But, Margaret—"

"No buts. You have to find a new job, that's all. Did your boss offer to give you a reference?"

"Yes, but he fired me, too."

"He did not fire you. He downsized his company. There's a big difference. You get yourself together, get out there tomorrow, and find another dream job."

Kathy nodded. "I know you're right. I do have to look again, but I don't want Ed to have to worry about all of this. He's so depressed a lot of the time anyway—and now this."

"I know. I've seen how down he is some days." Margaret thought a minute. "Kathy, you do have that two weeks' extra pay. Maybe you could wait a few days to tell Ed. By the time you have to tell him, you may already have another job."

Kathy shook her head. "I can't do that. He needs to know where I am in case something happens to Desmond. Besides, we tell each other everything. How can we pray together if we don't know what's happenin'?"

Margaret blushed, and she marveled again at this young woman's faith. "I'm sorry, Kathy. You're right. I just wanted to spare Ed some extra worry."

Kathy squared her shoulders. "I guess I just panicked for a few minutes. I really do appreciate you being here, but I know God will take care of us. I just lost sight of that for a little bit."

She reached over and hugged Margaret. "Thanks for being my friend."

Margaret shrugged. "No thanks needed, Kathy. You and Ed are the ones who are blessing me. Your faith amazes me, and I don't know whether I'll ever be able to trust as deeply as you two do."

Kathy grinned and hiccoughed again. "Sure, you will. Once you've seen God work the way we have, you may panic once in a while, but you can't ever forget. He's faithful in his promises."

After Kathy left, Margaret sat with her cup of tea and thought as she absently stroked Cat's ears. What did God have in mind for Kathy and Ed? How could they possibly meet everyday expenses like food and rent, let alone all of Ed's medical bills?

Her mind fumed. *What were you thinking, God?*

Chapter Twenty

*I*t was a couple of days before Margaret had the opportunity to check on Kathy and Ed. The morning she did call, Ed answered the phone.

"She's at work."

"Oh, Ed, that's wonderful! Where's she working?"

"At the McDonald's, down the street."

Margaret's heart sank. In two days, Kathy had gone from a well-paid secretary to a minimum-wage fast-food server. "Did she even try for another office job?"

"Oh, sure, and she's still tryin', but she was in Mickey D's the other day, and they had a sign out for people to open up the place. It's an early-morning shift, so she took it with the understanding she would be quittin' when she gets an office job. She's off by one in the afternoon, and as soon as she can she goes lookin' for somethin' else."

"Doesn't she get awfully tired?"

"Yeah, but she says we don't know how long it'll take to find anything, and this will at least keep the wolf from swallowin' us whole!"

"I suppose she's right," Margaret said, all the time envisioning the wolf already having consumed legs, torso, and arms. At this rate, it was only a matter of time before he snapped up their heads.

Ed interrupted her thoughts. "Micah came by this morning. He wants to teach me how to use the word processor on that computer Bruce gave us. Ain't that a laugh?"

"Why? Lots of men use computers every day. Maybe you could get hooked up to one of those free email servers, and you might be able to find some friends to keep you busy."

"You think so? I ain't never learned to type."

"You don't have to be fast, and as Micah told you, kids do it all the time. Your brain is still working."

"I dunno."

"Oh, give it a try, Ed. Who knows? You might really like it."

Micah called and came often during the next few weeks. He and Margaret frequently shared meals together. He helped her paint and decorate her flower pots, and pot the new little violet plants. They delivered them together, and talked and prayed with the nursing home residents.

At one time, Margaret had been repulsed at the idea of going to a nursing home, but when she sat with Micah and talked to these people, she realized how precious each one was. The women talked of family, and the men spoke of business and government changes they had witnessed, and at times, had a part in implementing. Margaret's visits became a joy, rather than an unpleasant duty. Days ran together, and Margaret went to church, came home, and worked on drapes for Mrs. Henderkind from church, took an order for some Priscilla sheers from Mrs. Whitson, and continued to fret over Kathy's lack of what Margaret viewed as a real job. How could God be so cruel as to let Kathy barely taste the benefits of a good job and snatch it away so quickly?

One afternoon, as she worked on Mrs. Henderkind's drapes, she listened to the local newscast on the television. Suddenly, she heard,

> ". . . Watson and Watson are undergoing an exten-
> sive investigation. There are allegations of fraud and
> interstate trade law violations. All employees with
> more than three month tenure are under investiga-
> tion and are subject to full prosecution . . ."

Margaret's mind froze, and she missed the rest of the report. Watson and Watson was the investment company Kathy had worked for. If Kathy had kept that job, she would have been dragged into that quagmire. Oh, praise God, she didn't have to cope with that on top of everything else she carried right now.

The moment the thought entered her mind, Margaret laid aside her sewing and bowed in humility. She truly prayed a prayer of thanksgiving, as opposed to the off-hand observation she had just made.

Even after all her angry thoughts and resentment over Kathy's loss of position, Margaret realized all honest work was honorable, and in his wisdom, God had allowed Kathy to be removed from harm's way. What a glorious God he truly was. She prayed her repentance and asked him to forgive her unbelief. She should have believed Micah and Kathy when they said, "God never breaks his promises."

She also reflected on the strength of Satan's devious ways of destroying one's relationship with God. She could see how Satan had used her temper and her self-reasoned sense of right and wrong to weaken her. In view of those reflections, she should not have been surprised when her phone rang a couple of weeks later.

"Mrs. Ceradsky? This is the owner of the baseball-card shop in Waynesville. I just found your card and remembered you were looking for Andy Bartimus. Did you ever find him?"

"No," Margaret croaked through her suddenly dry throat.

"Well, I saw this ad in one of the magazines with his name on it, and a box number in Olathe, Kansas. Ain't no phone number, but that's not too far from you, is it?"

"No," Margaret said. "No, only about thirty minutes away."

"Well, if you think the box number will help, I can give it to you."

Margaret grabbed up a pencil beside the phone and scribbled down the information.

"This ad has a bunch of stuff listed. Andy must be liquidating his whole collection. Anyways, I hope this helps you."

"Thank you," Margaret said. "I appreciate it."

Margaret hung up the phone and sat battling the war within her. She'd seen God's hand at work in Kathy's life, and she'd heard the story of the way He'd worked in Ed's and LaMont's lives, and in Bruce Jacobson's. She truly believed he worked for their good. And through the study she'd done with Micah, she could almost forgive Andy . . . but she'd searched a long time, and Olathe was so close.

She went to the phone and dialed directory assistance. "I'd like a number for Andrew Bartimus in Olathe, please."

"I'm sorry, I don't have a listing like that in Olathe."

"What about Overland Park or Kansas City proper?"

"I'm sorry, there's no listing for an Andrew, or an initial A. Bartimus in the whole metropolitan area."

"Thank you." Margaret hung up and stared at the phone.

She went upstairs to her desk and pulled out a piece of stationery.

Dear Mr. Bartimus,

I'm writing in response to your advertised baseball card collection. Could you please send me additional information, along with a phone number, so I can discuss terms with you?

Sincerely,

Margaret Miller

She felt a twinge of guilt at the deception, but her maiden name was Miller, and she hadn't really said she wanted to buy the cards, or which terms she wanted to discuss. If he drew the obvious conclusion, rather than the ones she intended, he could chalk it up to the inadequacies of the written word. But even as she stamped and mailed the envelope, a deep inner voice chastised her faulty thinking.

She walked back from the mailbox on the corner and heard her phone ringing when she unlocked her front door.

"Margaret," Kathy's voice fairly bubbled in her ear, "guess what?"

"What?"

"No, guess."

"Oh, Kathy, I'm no good at this. Desmond has a new tooth?"

"No. Something better."

"Ed can move his feet?"

"No!"

"So what? Tell me before I explode."

"I got a job. A real job!"

"That's great!" Margaret squealed, caught up in Kathy's excitement. "Where?"

"At one of the big phone companies. One of their executives comes into McDonald's for breakfast, and we got to visiting almost every day. He heard about the investigation at Watson and Watson, and I told him how glad I was I got out in time. He got sort of distant for a few days, but yesterday he came in and offered me the job."

"What changed him?"

"He told me he had someone run a background check on me, and they didn't find anything bad, so he asked if I wanted the job."

Margaret thought about Kathy's letdown over the loss of her job at Watson and Watson. "Does he know about Ed's history?"

"He didn't, but I told him."

Margaret groaned.

"No. It's okay. He said I could have kept it to myself, and he probably wouldn't have ever found out, but since I told him, he figures I must be honest and up front. He said I'm just the kind of person he wants working for him. And guess what?"

"Not again, Kathy. I'm really not good at this."

"I'll be making a dollar an hour more than I was at Watson and Watson!"

"Oh, wow!" Margaret exclaimed. "When God takes over, he really does it up right, doesn't He?"

"Don't you ever doubt it," Kathy said through her laughter.

Margaret felt her faith was stronger than it ever had been. She still wasn't sure she could totally control her anger at Andy, but it didn't consume every waking moment any longer.

"Guess what else?" Kathy said.

"Kathy?"

"Oh, okay. I'll tell you. Bruce has offered Ed a job!"

"What?"

"A job! He said now that Ed knows the computer keyboard, he could start some on-the-job training next week, if he wants the job. Can you imagine that? Of course he wants it!"

"That's great! What will his position be?"

"I don't know. Something to do with customer service, and get this: Bruce said Ed gets paid while he's in training. It's minimum wage 'til he finishes that, but then his salary will more than double, if he gets through it all."

"Is there any doubt?"

"Well, Bruce says it's tough, and about three out of seven don't finish, but the ones who do can advance to really good jobs. Ed doesn't need to be able to walk to do the job, either. Isn't it great?"

"Yes, Kathy." Margaret grabbed a tissue and blotted her eyes. Again. It seemed she was always crying, but now, hers were tears of joy, not tears of hurt and anger. "Yes, it's just like Bruce to do something like that, but he needs responsible people, and I'm sure he realizes what an asset Ed will be to his company."

"Yeah." Kathy's voice grew serious. "He will, won't he? That'll mean as much to Ed as the job. He needs to feel needed again."

As soon as Kathy hung up, Margaret dialed Micah's number. "Micah, have you heard about Ed's job?"

"Yes, as a matter of fact, I have."

"And you didn't tell me?"

"I couldn't. I was sworn to silence."

"Why? I mean, this is wonderful. Who could possibly object to the whole world knowing?"

"Nobody, now, but when I first heard about it, we didn't know whether it would work out or not."

Margaret's mind whirled. "When did you first know about it?"

"Before Ed's injury."

"Before—? How could that be?"

"Bruce talked to me about it a few weeks before Ed was shot, but Ed needed to learn to use a computer, and he didn't think he was smart enough. He'd resigned himself to a janitor's job for the rest of his life."

Margaret sputtered, "Of course, he's smart enough. Just look at him. But how did you change his mind about the job?"

"We didn't. We offered him a toy to appease his boredom."

"That didn't do much to get ready for a job."

"It got him past his fear of the computer. Then you gave him the desire to use email and that forced him to learn to type. The rest is history."

"Does Bruce think Ed can get through the training? Kathy says it's sort of tough."

"With the motivation Ed has, I don't see how he can fail—but if it looks like he might, Bruce intends to be his personal tutor. Ed will have a job if he really wants one."

Margaret started to chuckle, then she burst into full-blown laughter. "You guys are something. You're really something."

She heard Micah laugh, too, before he told her, "God works in mysterious ways his wonders to perform."

"With a lot of help from you and Bruce."

"He never said we couldn't help. In fact, Scripture says it's a sin to know to do good and not do it. Methinks this is a very good thing."

"Methinks you're right."

Margaret's love for Micah grew even more at that moment, and she found herself examining this whole series of events at all kinds of odd times over the next few days. God had been in control all along. Kathy didn't have to answer for a fraudulent boss, and Ed had been pushed into learning the skills he needed to get a much better job than he could have ever hoped to find as an unskilled ex-convict.

Margaret surrendered her heart to God totally, and decided she truly no longer wanted to exact any kind of revenge on Andrew Bartimus. If he deserved condemnation, the God who provided so well for Kathy and Ed could deal with punishment equally well. She told Micah her resolve, and he prayed with her and congratulated her on her growth. After all these months, at last Margaret had found true peace.

Until the afternoon Hank Arnold called her.

Chapter Twenty-one

"Mrs. Ceradsky? I just got a check in the mail for some stuff Andy Bartimus bought from me before he left Texas. Are you still looking for him?"

Margaret froze. Was she still looking for Andy? Was she a Christian or not? She really was willing to forgive and she expected to be forgiven. But did she still want to see Andy? She closed her eyes and swallowed.

"'Cause, if you are, he's in Kansas City. The return address on the envelope is a post office box number, but there's a Kansas City phone number here on the check, too."

Margaret forced her voice to work. "I see. Thank you for letting me know."

Hank read the number to her and wished her well. She hung up the phone and sank onto a kitchen chair.

"Oh, Lord, what do I do now?" She sat and thought and prayed until the room grew dusky. Cat came and brushed against her legs and mewed an urgent plea of hunger. Margaret rose and switched on the light and shook some cat chow into Cat's bowl.

She hated herself, but she picked up the phone and dialed the number. She had no idea what she would say when Andy answered, but it became a moot question, for the phone rang ten times with no response. Margaret slipped the receiver back on the hook.

"Thank you, God, and please continue to help me with this. I know my anger is still just below the surface, but I'm working on it. Really, I am."

When Micah came by the next afternoon, Margaret said, "I need to talk to you."

Micah gazed at her and seemed to grasp the intensity of her request. "What is it?" he asked.

Margaret led him to the living room, and when he had settled onto the sofa, and she in the flowered chair, she began. She told Micah about Hank's call, and how her anger had re-surfaced. She didn't try to excuse nor minimize the depth of her rage.

"I know as a Christian I can't exact punishment, and I think I've grown enough that I don't really want to any more, but I miss Angela, and I still hurt, and I'm still angry sometimes. Does that feeling ever go away?"

Micah sighed, took a shuddering breath, and said, "I don't know. I still miss Cora, and I still get angry when I think about what a terrible waste and injustice her death was. But I don't hate Ed anymore, and somehow I think that's the important thing.

"Jesus became enraged at the moneychangers at the temple, and he drove them out, but he didn't stay angry at the world, and he didn't slay them.

"Anger is one of the emotions God built into us, so in and of itself, I don't believe it's always wrong. What is wrong is what we do when we are angry. Do we use it to help build a better world, or do we use that adrenaline rush for destruction?"

Margaret nodded. "This Christianity stuff is hard."

"Yes, but it's worth the effort. Nobody promised a life of ease—even the apostles were martyred—but look at the final reward."

"I know, and I'm working on it."

"Want to pray about it?"

"Yes. Yes, I think I need all the help I can get."

Micah's prayer washed over her and gripped Margaret's heart. She wanted to do God's will, and she knew with Micah and God helping her, she could. Her tears of remorse ran freely before God's peace settled upon her.

She didn't call Andy's number again.

Margaret continued to study her Bible over the following weeks, and she watched Mack Lyon's program regularly. Her faith grew stronger, and when she was honest with herself, she admitted, so did her love for Micah. The beautiful part of the whole situation was, she knew his love for her was growing, too.

It had happened slowly, and gently, but now her love was strong, and it felt so good to experience love again. She felt her recovery was almost complete, and she knew Micah's love for her was more than that of one Christian for another. He called her almost every day with an invitation to go somewhere with him, or just to talk.

They went to visit Ed, and other members of the congregation who were ill or shut-in. They went to the nursing home. They went to the hospital. They went to dinner. And they went to church together. And they talked, and they studied, and they prayed. They had spent so much time together, they began to correctly second guess one another's sentence endings and actions.

Margaret smiled as she thought about it. Micah had even developed a relationship with Cat. Anyone who knew anything at all about feline behavior knew cats develop an affinity for one person they prefer, and merely tolerate the rest of humanity. But not Cat. Cat loved Margaret and Micah equally. Margaret was sure it had to do with some animals being able to sense a person's inner heart. She was sure Cat knew Micah's heart was pure and kind.

She glanced down at the get well cards Micah had asked her to address. He had been called to the hospital to sit with someone, and he'd asked her to be sure these got in the mail today.

She met the mailman at the box and took the handful of envelopes he offered her in return. She went to the kitchen table and flipped through the stack. Her hand froze. There, among the bills, was an envelope with a return address headed, A. Bartimus.

Her hand trembled when she laid it aside. She didn't look at it again until Micah came that evening.

She took him to the kitchen and poured out the story of how she came to have the box number and what she'd done with it. When she finished, perspiration dampened her brow, and tears lurked at the corners of her eyes.

Micah remained silent for several long seconds, then he asked, "Do you still want to harm Andy?"

Margaret started to say yes, for when she had mailed that letter, she had. She'd still wanted to destroy Andy—but now—now, she wasn't so sure. She knew as a Christian she shouldn't, but sitting here in front of Micah, she didn't find the answer so readily as she had only a couple of weeks ago.

Finally, she said, "I don't know. I don't think so, but sometimes I still get so angry, it scares me."

Micah nodded. "I know. I feel it too, at times."

Margaret searched Micah's face and looked deep into his eyes. She believed him, but how did he reconcile that anger and the way she knew he felt toward Ed now?

"I don't understand."

"Have you prayed about it any more?"

"Yes, a lot."

"Has it helped?"

"It did, or at least I thought it did, until today." She reached over to the counter and picked up the envelope. "I was sure I had it under control, until this came."

She handed the white packet with an Olathe box number for the return address to Micah.

"That's my answer to the letter I sent two weeks ago. I've been afraid to open it. Micah, I want to do what's right, but I can't seem to turn the past loose, and I think maybe I could, if I could just see and talk to Andy."

"You still need a confrontation?"

"No, not a confrontation—just a sharing of memories, maybe." She pushed her hands through her hair. "I don't know—I—maybe it is a confrontation I want."

Micah didn't say anything. He just sat and waited for Margaret to continue.

"Micah, I need to know where he is. I'm trying to keep my emotions in control and do what God would expect, but I need some answers. Would you open the envelope for me?"

Micah studied her, then nodded and tore the flap open. Even before he pulled the sheet of paper out, he said, "Margaret, sometimes the answers we seek aren't really satisfying. It's the good things we experience that fulfill our needs."

Margaret couldn't force an answer through her lips.

Micah unfolded the paper and held it out to her. She shrank away from it. "Would you read it to me?"

He drew it back and scanned it quickly before he said, "It's a form letter."

> Dear Collector,
>
> Thank you for your inquiry. The response to my ad has been tremendous, and unfortunately, before I received your request, the entire collection sold.
>
> Again, thank you, and good luck finding what you're seeking.
>
> Sincerely,
>
> Andrew Bartimus

Margaret sank back against the chair back, closed her eyes, and sighed deeply. "Another dead end."

Micah smiled. "Maybe you're not supposed to find him."

Margaret nodded. "At least, not yet. Maybe by the time I do I won't feel such a need to see him anymore."

Micah shook his head and gave a sad little smile. "Don't count on it."

Margaret sewed, baby-sat with Desmond occasionally, and saw Micah almost daily over the next several weeks. She watched Ed and Kathy adapt to their new jobs, and the joy they radiated was unbelievable. Margaret could hardly believe how such a short time ago things had seemed so hopeless, and now the young couple faced a future with financial challenges, but certainly with hope.

Each time they arose, Margaret forced thoughts of Angela's death from her mind and concentrated on the task of living. Gradually her anger diminished.

One afternoon, late in August, Micah brought her back from a trip to the nursing home.

"Come in and have a soda," Margaret invited. "It's hot enough to boil eggs in the sun."

"Sounds good."

They entered the kitchen, and Margaret punched the message button on her answering machine on her way to the refrigerator.

"Mrs. Ceradsky, this is Sam Hilton. I'm the guy from the baseball shop in Waynesville, again. I got another, older, magazine here with an ad by Andy Bartimus. It lists his house number in Olathe." He read off the specific address, then said, "I hope this helps."

Margaret froze, then glanced up at Micah. "I haven't talked to that man since last spring. Why couldn't he have lost my number?"

"I don't know," Micah said, "but he didn't, and now you have to make a decision."

"I know . . . I know I should just forget this . . . but I need to see Andy. I need to talk to him. I don't want to punish him anymore, but I need to see him."

"Would it help if I go with you?"

Margaret paused, then nodded. "Yes. It would help a lot, but are you sure you want to?"

"I'll always want to be beside you," Micah said with a sincerity Margaret could not mistake for flippancy.

They drove to the address Sam had specified. The house had been nice at one time, but now it needed paint. A window in the garage door was cracked, and one length of the guttering sagged. The house suffered from obvious neglect.

They rang the doorbell, but nobody answered. Just as they turned to leave, a lady stepped out of the house next door. She walked to her driveway and picked up her newspaper.

"You folks lookin' for Andy?"

"Yes. Do you happen to know when we could catch him home?" Micah asked.

"Ain't likely to for quite a while. He's spendin' all his time at the hospital these days."

Margaret started to ask which hospital, but the woman rushed on.

"His little girl's got leukemia, and they're givin' her some kind of new treatment. They say they can expect complete remission when she finishes up. Be a real blessin' when they're done, but it sure is hard on both of 'em right now, what with Andy havin' them colds and flu all the time."

Margaret glanced at Micah and frowned. People got colds every day. It was hay fever season, too. He could just have a bad allergy— or a whole group of them, or he could be really sick.

"Do you know which hospital the little girl is in?" Margaret asked.

"Children's Mercy, last I knew. Best kid's hospital in the country."

Micah asked, "Her name's Quinthia? Is that right?"

"Yeah, that's her name. You folks not family, then?"

"No," Margaret said. "Andy and my daughter were friends. I'm looking him up because of her."

The woman eyed them suspiciously. "Well, if you wanna see him, ya best go to Mercy. Only time he's home is late at night, once in a while."

"Thanks. We'll do that," Micah said. He took Margaret's elbow and steered her to the car.

Once inside, he turned to her. "So, what do you want to do?"

She clenched her hands in a knot in her lap, then whispered, "Go to the hospital."

Margaret was thankful Micah drove in silence. He didn't preach or try to change her mind. But her insides twisted. They ground and gurgled, and a vise squeezed her chest. Micah didn't have to say anything. His silence convicted her more completely than his words ever could have.

He stopped at the toll gate and took a ticket, then when the gate opened, pulled into a parking space only a few steps from the entry to the hospital. He started to get out when Margaret laid her hand on his arm.

"Micah, thank you so much for being here. I just want to tell you before we go in that this is no longer about revenge. I think I can finally truly say I don't wish Andy any harm, but I still need to see him."

Micah patted her hands. "I'm so glad you've worked this through, and I wouldn't be anywhere else. I knew you couldn't hold your anger forever. I've seen you grow too much. You may still have times when things get rough, but remember, I'm here to help, and God will never leave you."

She smiled. "I know." She squeezed the hands that held hers—those big, strong, yet gentle hands that seemed to always be there to lift her up.

Micah pulled her along. "Let's go find Andy and Quinthia."

At the front desk, the receptionist directed them to the east wing on an upper floor. They started down the hall.

"Wait," Margaret said, and she turned back to the receptionist. "Where's the gift shop?"

They followed the directions and Margaret rushed in and searched the displays. At last, she found a soft, plush teddy bear and carried it to the cashier.

"Every little girl needs a cuddly bear," she explained feebly.

Micah only grinned.

Margaret felt that now-familiar squeeze around her heart before she turned toward the elevators.

At the appropriate stop, they stepped out into an open play area. A nurses' station was a few feet away. Margaret walked over and asked where to find Quinthia's room.

"It's the end one, down that way, but I think her daddy has her in the TV room. It's that way." She pointed. "They're the only ones in there right now."

Margaret thanked her and turned to go where the woman had indicated.

"Would you rather I waited here?" Micah asked, pointing to a comfortable-looking chair.

"It might be best," Margaret said. "I don't want to embarrass him."

It almost surprised her to hear those words come from her mouth. Only a few weeks ago, she had wanted to do a lot more than embarrass Andrew Bartimus.

She had wanted to crush him—not to death, for that would have ended his humiliation. She had wanted him to suffer every degradation and defeat she, or anyone else, could conjure up. But now all she wanted was to meet him—again. To see him, and see if she could ease his pain in any way.

She stopped at the door to the room where she knew she would at last find Andy and his little girl. It startled her even more than it would have anyone else that she wanted to help Andy.

Until this very moment, the idea had never presented itself—even in her "you ought to" thoughts, those self talks where she scolded: You ought to get on with your life . . . You ought to forgive . . . You ought to give up your search. But never once had she ever told herself, you ought to help him.

But, here and now, standing at this door, she knew she had to help, if there was any way. She couldn't do anything else.

She squared her shoulders, clutched the new teddy bear to her breast, and stepped through the door.

Chapter Twenty-two

Margaret was not prepared for the sight before her. Andy sat in a rocking chair across the room. She recognized his facial features, but he looked so thin, almost like someone had formed a man from strands of pasta. Two *el dente* strands wrapped snugly around the little girl in his lap.

Margaret recognized the look, and she fought tears. She knew Andy was dying. From the looks of him, it would be a very short time before he would lose his struggle for life.

The little girl in his lap was bald, save a few short wisps of new black growth. She was wrapped in a fuzzy blanket, but her face looked full, and her deep brown eyes shone bright.

Margaret's heart melted. Even bald, this child was beautiful.

"Andy?" she asked. "Andy Bartimus?"

Andy turned, question in his expression.

She stepped forward. "I'm Margaret Ceradsky. I don't know whether you remember me or not, but I'm Angela's mother."

Quinthia jerked the blanket up over her head so that only her eyes peered out. Margaret's heart ached. Even at her tender age, Quinthia was embarrassed by her loss of hair.

Andy shifted Quinthia and struggled to rise. "Of course I remember you."

"Don't get up," Margaret hurried to say. "You seem to have quite a lapful." She smiled at the little girl.

"Yes, I do. This is my daughter Quinthia."

Margaret held out her hand. "Hello, Quinthia. I'm Margaret."

Quinthia stared at the hand but didn't offer to take it. She would have had to relinquish her hold on the blanket. She did offer a shy "Hi."

Margaret stooped. "How are you feeling?"

"Yucky!"

165

Margaret glanced over at the basin nearby. She knew many of the cancer treatments made the patients violently ill. "I'm sorry to hear that, but maybe tomorrow will be better."

"Nope," the little girl said matter-of-factly. "Not 'til next week. Then Dr. Sultaneyia says I can go home."

"That's good," Margaret said. "But in the meantime, do you think a special purple cheer-me-up bear would help?"

Quinthia eyed the bear Margaret held up. "One with a red bow?" she asked.

"Yes," Margaret answered. "A red bow just like this one, and brown shoes like these."

"And a green vest?"

"Um hum, just like this one." She held out the toy.

Quinthia forgot to hold the blanket and reached out. She took the bear and hugged him. "Nope. I don't feel no better. . . but he could keep me company."

Margaret nodded. "I think he would like that a lot."

Quinthia pulled the bear under the blanket. "Is his name Winston?"

Margaret said seriously, "I don't know. I didn't ask him his name. Why don't you?"

Quinthia nodded. "His name's Winston, all right."

She snuggled down in Andy's lap. "I'm tired, Daddy."

"Then go to sleep, sweetie. I'll rock you."

He began a gentle rock, and looked at Margaret. "How'd you find us? We've moved so many times, even family has a hard time keeping up with us."

Margaret made a quick decision. Andy didn't need to know how diligently she had searched, or why.

"I know. I talked to your class reunion committee when they were looking for you, and to make a long story short, someone I contacted at that time called me the other day after they saw your baseball card ads in some magazine."

"Oh, yeah. They ran quite a while. I quit even checking the post office box. We've been here all week."

"How's her treatment doing?"

"It should end next week, and if her tests turn out okay, we should be able to go home."

He coughed and Margaret noticed how he gasped often between words. Quinthia might be well enough to go home, but she wasn't so sure about Andy.

After a long pause, Andy said, "I'm really sorry about Angela." He didn't look up from where he picked at a bit of lint on Quinthia's blanket.

His statement ripped at Margaret. She swallowed and struggled for composure. "She died last spring," she said softly.

Andy ducked his head. "I'm sorry," he said softly. He coughed again. "I know how much that hurts. My wife died three years ago, and not long ago I lost Quinthia's twin brother." He lifted a hand in despair. "Now, she's sick."

His voice trailed off, but then a tiny smile lifted the corners of his mouth, and he spoke again. "But the doctor says Quinthia should go into remission after this treatment, and she could live to a ripe old age. They're doing lots of research, and a cure for leukemia is just around the corner."

"Good," Margaret said. "I'm really glad."

The room grew silent save the sound of the children's cartoon on the television.

Andy looked up. "What happened to Angela?"

Margaret no longer felt the urge to scream or claw at Andy. All she felt was a deep sense of sorrow that this terrible tragedy had gone so far.

"She died of AIDS, Andy."

She watched his face crumple, and she wanted to hold him and comfort him, the way he held and comforted Quinthia. She tried to swallow the lump in her throat.

"I loved her, you know? I asked her to marry me, but she wouldn't."

Margaret's head jerked up, and before she could stop herself, she blurted, "I don't believe you!"

Andy gazed at her so long she swallowed, opened her mouth to speak, but no sound came out, so she clamped her lips together and stood and stared at this audacious man.

"I truly did love her. We dated quite a while before you ever knew. Angela told you she was going to spend the night with friends, and she did, but we'd double date first."

"Why would she do that? I let her date."

"Sure—with the local guys, but she knew you didn't want her to date any of the guys from the base."

And I was right! Her head throbbed. *If she'd stayed away from you, she'd still be alive.*

She tried to keep her voice low. As angry as she was, she didn't want to distress the child. "The boys on base moved away and left the girls in emotional shreds. I didn't want Angela hurt like that."

Andy frowned and shifted a sleepy Quinthia into a more comfortable position. "I was the one left in shreds."

Margaret stared, speechless.

He continued. "Angela and I didn't date near as long as I wanted to, but I knew I loved her." He swallowed. "That night after graduation, we both lost our heads. It only happened once, but I wanted to marry her."

Margaret's eyes filled with tears. "She said it was a date rape."

Andy glared at his hands. "Maybe it was," he said, finally. "It didn't feel like it at the time. I thought she loved me, too. She told me she did, but later, when I called her, she wouldn't talk to me, and she wouldn't see me. It was like I had leprosy. I didn't know it then, but I was even worse than that. Then Dad got transferred, and I eventually met my wife."

Margaret sat silent. Did she believe Andy? If what he said was true, why didn't he try to contact Angela when he found out he had AIDS?

As if he read her thoughts, he continued. "I tried to call last year, but your phone isn't listed anymore, and the kids took all my time, especially when they both got sick."

Margaret had never considered Andy might try to reach Angela.

She had the phone unlisted when they started receiving hang-up calls at all hours of the day and night during Angela's illness. Some self-righteous soul's idea of justice, she supposed.

"You're dying now, too, aren't you?" she asked.

Andy nodded. "Yes. I may have another six months, if the weather doesn't get cold too early. I've had pneumonia once, and the next time it'll probably take me."

He didn't sound bitter, only deeply sorrowful in his resignation. "My greatest goal is to find a good home for Quinthia before I die. I need somebody who knows how to pray for that."

Margaret nodded. "Andy, a friend of mine is outside. He's a minister. Would you like for me to have him come in and pray with us?"

"Do you think he would? I mean—I'm not sure I have any right to pray."

"Maybe not, but Micah does, and he knows what to tell you about how to get your life in order so you can pray. If you're willing, he can teach you all about how to claim your share of the treasures laid up in heaven."

Margaret could hardly believe her own ears. She was barely more than a babe in Christ herself, and here she was telling Andy Bartimus —Andy Bartimus, of all people—how to get to heaven.

"I'd like to meet him," Andy said.

Margaret went to the door and motioned for Micah. When he reached her, she said softly, "Andy's dying. He wants us to pray for Quinthia's future, and I told him you could tell him about salvation."

Micah laid his arm lightly across her shoulder and squeezed. "Good girl. Let's go help this young man find some peace."

Margaret introduced Micah, and they prayed. Then Micah talked to Andy about an exacting God who required repentance from sin, and a loving God who provided the sacrifice for those same sins, so that nobody except Jesus had to pay the horrible price each one owes. He spoke of the first sermon Peter preached where guilty men cried out, "Men and brethren, what shall we do?" and Peter told them to "repent and be baptized for the remission of sins." He assured Andy that he, too, could be free from sin.

Andy shook his head. "I don't deserve that kind of forgiveness."

Margaret knew he was right. He didn't deserve it, but now, after all this time, she realized even more deeply, neither had she. At one time she had wanted Andy to burn in hell. Now it was vital that he understand he didn't have to.

She leaned over and placed her hands on Andy's bony knees. His time to decide was short. Already he was wasting away. "If any of us deserved forgiveness, it wouldn't have been necessary for Jesus to die. Only undeserving people need his sacrifice—and we are all undeserving."

"I'll think about it," he said.

"But—" Margaret said.

"He needs time to work this through," Micah said gently. "This is not a decision one makes lightly."

Margaret stood. "You're right. It shouldn't be a snap decision."

She picked up her purse. "I think we should go now, but if it's okay, we'll come again."

"That would be nice," Andy said.

He glanced down at Quinthia, who lay asleep on his lap. "Thank you for the gift. She loves teddy bears, and her favorite one disintegrated in the washer a few days ago. She wouldn't accept any other substitute, but she seems to like this one."

"Oh, good," Margaret said. She chuckled. "He was the most outrageously dressed one I saw. I know how radical little girls can be. He just seemed like the right choice at the time."

Andy smiled. "I guess that's sort of fitting. This whole situation is outrageous."

Of course Andy was right, but how could Margaret comment without doing more harm?

Chapter Twenty~three

*I*n the car, Margaret leaned back against the seat and closed her eyes. She was emotionally drained. She prayed earnestly that Andy would recognize his need for God soon. He was so frail; she knew he didn't have much time left to make any decisions.

He had mentioned a home for Quinthia. She wondered if anyone was already working on that. She knew they should be. Something like that took time for a sound child, and for one as sick as Quinthia, it could take an indeterminate time. She knew there were good people willing to take ill children, but they weren't plentiful. What would happen to that sweet little girl?

Margaret heard the crunch of gravel beneath the car, and she felt it roll to a stop. She opened her eyes, and looked around. "Where are we?"

Micah turned in his seat. "Waterworks Park. You can see the city from here. I come here every so often to pray or to meditate on some problem. It's quiet here."

Margaret glanced around at the small park. Theirs was the only car there. In the distance, she could indeed see where the Missouri River would roll along below the bluff where downtown Kansas City perched. It was dark, and the lights in the buildings twinkled bright cheer across the horizon.

"It's beautiful," she said. She leaned back again, and they sat in companionable silence.

Micah waited a few moments, then said, "I thought you might need to talk about your feelings over the evening's developments."

Margaret bit her lower lip. Snippets of conversation whirled through her brain. "He said he didn't rape her."

Micah sat silent. Margaret didn't know what she expected him to say, but she knew she was in no mood for platitudes.

"Then he said maybe Angela thought it was rape."

171

She swallowed and grabbed a tissue from her purse to blot her tears and catch the drip from her nose. "He said he loved her. If he loved her so much, why didn't he try harder to see her, or something? Why did he just move off and leave her?"

Micah remained silent and let her think and talk.

"He didn't write. Not once. I would have seen the letters."

She twisted the tissue into a knot. "Stupid kids. They were so young, they didn't even know what love is."

She pulled another tissue from her purse and blew her nose again. "Micah, I'm really trying not to hate Andy, and part of the time I'm okay, but other times, I still want to pound him to a bloody pulp."

Micah took her into his arms and let her sob on his shoulder. "I know," he said, "but given time, it will get better. The best way I know is to first pray about it, and then spend some time with Andy and Quinthia. It's hard to hate someone you know well."

When Micah dropped her off a little later, he pulled her close and kissed her. "You'll work it out," he said.

Here in Micah's arms she believed she could. With God helping, and with Micah by her side, Margaret did believe she could cope with almost anything. She snuggled into Micah's embrace and let him kiss her again. Yes, in Micah's arms the whole world looked right.

Margaret wasn't sure spending time with Andy would work the healing she sought, but she could see no other cure, so she decided to try Micah's suggestion.

The first thing she did the next morning was visit a fabric shop and buy a pattern for little girls' hats. She quickly selected a print fabric with tiny pigs, one with teddy bears, and one with blue and white stripes.

As soon as she paid for her selections, she rushed home. She went straight to her sewing room and spread the prints on the cutting board. She wanted to finish at least one of the hats before Micah came by that evening. She resolutely ignored Cat's antics and was tacking the bow in place when her doorbell rang.

She carried the hat in her hand when she rushed to let Micah in. "Hi," she said, and leaned over for Micah's kiss.

"Hi, yourself," he said before he kissed her on the cheek. "Hi, Cat."
He stroked Cat's length, then asked, "Whatcha got?"

Margaret held up the little hat. "Something for Quinthia. She's
awfully self-conscious over her lack of hair. I thought she might like
this. I'm sure somewhere along the line Locks of Love will be available to Quinthia, but in the meantime, I made her a hat."

Micah looked puzzled. "Locks of Love?"

"Yes. It's a group dedicated to providing wigs for cancer patients.
Many women grow their hair especially for the project. When it gets
long enough to spare at least nine inches, they go to the beauty shop
and have it cut and sent to Locks of Love. They take it and make the
wigs."

"That's very generous. It takes most women a long time to grow
hair that long."

"Yes, but I know even young girls who have done it more than
once. Until Quinthia gets a wig, though, I'll take her the hat."

"Good idea."

He looked at her and accused, "You've been sewing all afternoon.
You haven't had dinner yet, have you?"

"No, but we need to go to the hospital."

"Yes, we do, but you need to eat, too."

"You've been to dinner, and I can wait 'til later."

"Get your purse, and let's go," Micah said. "And you might need
a sweater. It's getting cooler."

Margaret grabbed a bag and tucked the hat inside, then went for
her purse and sweater.

Micah drove straight to the drive-through at Burger King and
asked, "What do you want?"

Margaret smiled. "Bully! I'll have a burger and a vanilla milk
shake, thank you."

Just before they walked into Quinthia's room at the hospital,
Micah said, "Give me the hat."

"Why?"

"Just give it to me."

Margaret handed him the bag, and he took out the hat and handed the sack back.

He perched the much-too-small hat atop his gray hair. "Let's go."

"Micah?"

"Come on," he insisted as he took her arm and knocked on the door.

"Come in," Andy said.

They pushed the door open and stepped inside. Quinthia had a towel pulled around her head and pinched tight under her chin.

Andy sat beside her bed, a Dr. Seuss book open on his lap.

"Daddy, look!" Quinthia squealed and giggled. "Look at his funny hat."

Micah whirled around as though looking for the hat. "Where?"

"There." She pointed. "On your head."

Micah reached up and patted the hat. "Oh, dear. I forgot. I put that up there intending to take it to some little girl who would love a piggy hat. Do you know anyone who could use a herd of pigs like this?"

"Me," Quinthia squealed. "Me!"

"You? Why, I bet you have hundreds of hats."

"Huh ugh. I don't gots none."

"None?"

"Nope."

"W-e-e-l-l-l-l," Micah held the hat and examined it closely, "it does look like it might fit you. Do you want to try it on?"

"Yeah," she shrieked.

Micah grinned broadly and handed her the hat. "Do you have a mirror in there somewhere?" He indicated the bedside table.

Andy tilted the over-the-bed tabletop to expose a mirror.

"Look, Daddy!" Quinthia preened. "Look. It fits."

"It does, doesn't it? Maybe you should say thank you."

"Thank you, thank you, thank you," Quinthia chanted as she tilted her head first one way and then the other to examine her reflection.

"Don't thank me," Micah said. "Thank this lady. She's the one who made it. I just modeled it for you."

Quinthia's eyes grew huge when she turned to Margaret. "You did? You really made this for me?"

"Yes, dear, I did," Margaret said. She was so pleased that Quinthia had been spared a lengthy embarrassing explanation about the hat's true purpose. Micah may never have had children, but he certainly had handled this situation well.

Quinthia broke into her thoughts. "Would you read me the story 'bout the three pigs? Daddy has it over there." Quinthia pointed at a stack of books on the window ledge.

"Sure. Why don't I do that while your daddy and Micah go talk?"

"Okay."

Andy handed Margaret the book. "You sure you'll be okay?" he asked his daughter.

"Yes." Quinthia's tone was full of chastisement. "I'm a big girl."

Margaret didn't miss Andy's melancholy. "Yes, you are, sweetie. I'll be right out there in the waiting room if you need me."

"I know." Quinthia dismissed him with a long-suffering glance.

Margaret ran a quick prayer through her mind and flipped the book to the first page. "Once upon a time, there were three little pigs . . ."

When Andy and Micah returned to the room, Margaret glanced at her watch. The two men had talked almost two hours, and Quinthia lay sound asleep on her bed.

"Has she had her shots, yet?" Andy asked.

"Yes, they came a while ago. She took them like a little trooper, then she went right off to sleep."

"Yes, they always make her sleepy."

"So how did your talk go?"

"Okay," Andy said. "Micah has helped me learn a good bit about God and how he works. I have a lot to think about."

Margaret wanted to reach over and click Andy's mind on high speed. If he was going to accept God's gracious gift of salvation, he would need to do it soon.

On the other hand, at the back of her mind, she knew she wouldn't be overly upset if Andy did not reconcile himself to God. She knew she shouldn't feel that way, and she squelched those impulses every time they arose—but they still popped up at the least little opportunity. She knew she had to continue to battle the rage within her.

Margaret watched Andy's hands droop between his legs in weariness as he leaned forward in his chair. His shoulders sagged as though the entire universe rested there. Compassion swelled in her, for she remembered—oh, how she remembered—how it felt to sit by and watch her only child waste away. Once she had wished for this. Once it had been the only thing driving her. But now it broke her heart. She was on the emotional roller coaster again.

"Andy, you need some rest. Why don't you go home and try to sleep. I'll stay with Quinthia tonight."

He looked up and stared at her a long moment. Margaret wondered if he questioned her motives, or her ability.

Before she could say anything, Andy said, "She's usually really sick a couple of hours after her injections. It's not pleasant."

"I know."

Andy glanced up, and Margaret could see the hurt in his eyes. "I guess you do, don't you?"

"Yes, and there are nurses to help, if we need them."

"I don't want to leave without telling her. I'll have to wait 'til she wakes up."

Micah propped against the wide window ledge and looked down at the large reclining rocker Margaret occupied.

"I could go ask for another chair," Andy said.

"Don't bother," Micah said. "If my calculations are right, and your estimate of a couple of hours are accurate, Quinthia should be awake soon."

"Unfortunately for her, you're right." Andy leaned back on the straight-backed chair.

"You don't realize how much I appreciate the offer of a respite. I need a shower, and sleep has been almost a non-entity this past couple of weeks."

Margaret bit her lips just in time to keep from saying, "I remember." She didn't want to punish Andy any more. His anguish was as much as she could have ever hoped, and there was no joy in seeing it at all. In fact, her heart ached for him, because she did know the overwhelming weariness, the despair, the frustration, and the totally helpless feelings Andy experienced.

Quinthia began to whimper, then suddenly, sat upright and cried, "Daddy!"

Andy and Margaret both lunged for the basin, and both were too late.

Quinthia sobbed. "I sorry—Daddy—I sorry."

Margaret hurried to her side. "It's okay, baby. Here, hold the basin in case you need it again, and I'll ring the nurse to get you some clean sheets."

Andy opened the bedside table. "There're some clean gowns here."

Micah had backed toward the door making soft gagging noises.

Margaret chuckled. "Micah, would you bring us a warm washcloth from the bathroom?"

"Certainly," he said as he rushed across the room.

Margaret quickly folded the sheet over itself to cover the mess. She hoped it would help Micah not to see it, and he would be better under control by the time he came back.

Much to her relief, in a moment he handed her the requested cloth, and he seemed fine. At least he'd quit making odd noises. Margaret sponged Quinthia down and started to help her change her gown.

"Don't take my hat off," Quinthia said before she pulled it down tighter on her head with both hands.

"I wouldn't dream of it," Margaret assured her. "Those pigs belong up there, and they might get lost if we set them off your head."

"Yeah," Quinthia said. "Losted pigs are not good."

"Right you are," Margaret said, all the while pulling arms out and pushing them back into gown sleeves.

By the time the nurse came, the only thing left to do was change the sheets. As soon as that was done and Quinthia was settled back in bed, Andy said, "You acted like a pro."

Margaret grinned and patted his hand. "We'll cope just fine." She nodded at Quinthia. "You want to tell her good-bye 'til sometime tomorrow? As you can see, she's in good hands."

"Yes to both counts," Andy said, and he turned to Quinthia. "Feel better now?"

"Um hum." Quinthia squirmed down under the blanket, but she made sure the hat remained in place, and Winston lay close by.

"Quinthia, Margaret has offered to stay with you tonight while Daddy goes home and takes care of some things there. Would that be okay with you?"

"Are you coming back?"

Margaret's heart stopped. Of course, Andy would be back this time, but someday soon, he wouldn't. Dear God in heaven, she dreaded that day, and Quinthia needed his help to prepare for it.

Chapter Twenty-four

"I'll be back in the morning, honey, if that's okay with you. You should go back to sleep soon, and Margaret will be here all night in case you need anything. Okay?"

Quinthia turned to Margaret. "Will you read me the funny cat book?"

"Which book is that?" Margaret asked, thumbing through the volumes on the window ledge.

"The hat book."

"Ah, *The Cat in the Hat?*"

"Yeah. That one."

"I think that could be arranged, but tell your daddy bye first, and I'll come and sit close to the bed so you can see the pictures."

"Goody! Bye, Daddy," Quinthia said without a second glance in her father's direction.

A rather abashed looking Andy came to kiss his daughter and say, "Bye to you, too." He chuckled, then turned to Margaret. "She should be okay 'til tomorrow, when they do it again."

Margaret nodded. "We'll be fine either way," she said.

Micah stood, "Andy, you look really beat. Why don't you let me drive you home. I can pick you up in the morning before I come to get Margaret."

"I don't want you to have to do that. I live at the opposite corner of the city from you."

"I would rather drive you than worry all night about whether or not you made it home. You're dead on your feet."

He threw his arm across Andy's shoulder. "Come on. You can tell me all about Quinthia on the way home."

The two men left the room, and Margaret heard Andy say, "If you're sure."

She was glad Micah had offered. She remembered some times

179

she'd driven home from the hospital while Angela was ill, and the next day being unable to remember the trip. Micah could spare Andy that danger, at least this one time.

Things went well for, as Andy said, Quinthia settled down and slept the remainder of the night. Thanks to the reclining rocker, Margaret was able to lean far back in the seat, and she slept remarkably well, considering the noise on the hospital ward.

The next night, after Quinthia got past her ill period, Micah volunteered to stay.

"I don't know," Andy said in a doubtful tone. "Quinthia doesn't usually get sick more than once after a treatment, but once in a while she has two or three rounds of nausea before she calms down."

Micah shrugged. "So, I may throw up with her, but we'll get by. You and Margaret both need some sleep, and I'll cope."

Margaret beamed. She knew how hard it was for Micah to cope with this particular situation, but he was determined, and she loved him for it more than he would ever realize.

The week passed with Micah, Margaret, and Andy alternating nights with Quinthia. Margaret grew to love the little girl more each time she saw her. Margaret watched Micah joke and laugh and talk of plans to take Quinthia to see a children's attraction called Kaleidoscope, the petting zoo, Worlds of Fun, or Penguin Park in the northern end of the city.

"Can Winston go, too?" Quinthia asked, her eyes glittering with excitement.

"Of course. We can't go anywhere without Winston. But you have to get well first."

Margaret's heart ached when Quinthia told Micah, "But I don't like shots."

Micah frowned. "You know what?"

"What?" Quinthia asked, her lip protruded into a pout.

"I don't like shots either, but if they made me well enough to go to Kaleidoscope, I think I could handle a few more."

"But they hurt!"

"Would it help if Winston hugged and kissed you after every one?"

Quinthia thought a moment. "Maybe, but they'd still hurt."

"Yes, they would," Micah agreed, "but you could take Winston home one of these days, and he wouldn't have to live in this hospital. Did you know he's never lived outside this room?"

"He hasn't?" Quinthia's eyes widened in wonder.

"Nope, and just think how he'll like the sunshine and the swings. He's never even seen a slide."

"Yeah," Quinthia sighed. "Swings and slides are nice."

"Yeah," Micah agreed.

Every day Micah thought up some new adventure they could explore as soon as Quinthia got better. Margaret was delighted at how well the two responded to one another. Who would have thought a childless man could develop such rapport with a three-year-old little girl?

The fury rushed back when Margaret stepped onto the ward and smelled the heavy scent of antiseptics. Blind rage engulfed her any time she allowed herself to think of how short Quinthia's life might be. At those times it took all Margaret's resolve to turn away from those feelings and think on other things. She often recited to herself: "Whatsoever things are pure, whatsoever things are lovely . . . think on these things."

Micah often went to the hospital with Margaret, and he frequently interrupted her meditations with a hug or a pat. It seemed as though he could peer into her mind and tell when she struggled most.

There had been a time when the very idea of being so transparent would have terrified Margaret, but now she found Micah's perception a definite comfort. He seemed to be able to read her nuances of mood at times even more accurately than she.

After one particularly trying afternoon, Micah led her to the car and headed home, but rather than take the Paseo bridge, he headed across the Heart of America crossing. Margaret knew he must be headed back to Waterworks Park, so she leaned back, closed her eyes, and let her mind search out peaceful thoughts.

When Micah parked, she opened her eyes and smiled at him. "I've begun to enjoy this place almost as much as you do."

"I'm glad. There have been days when a few minutes here were all that kept me sane."

Margaret studied Micah a moment. "I know what you mean. You realize I'm still struggling over Andy, don't you."

"Yes, but I have no doubt you'll work it out. You've come too far to drop the ball now."

"Do you really think so?"

"I know so." He took her hand into his and patted it gently. "Your innate goodness won't let you do anything else."

"Ah, but my inner war goes on."

"You'll win. You have God, and me, on your side."

"I hope so. Without you two, I don't know where I'd be."

"That brings me to a point—"

"Micah, do we have to talk?"

"No. I suppose not, for a while anyway."

The silence grew long, but Margaret leaned back and closed her eyes and let the peacefulness of the moment wash over her. She sat a long time, and gradually her spirit calmed. She even felt like smiling again. She continued to meditate until Micah broke the silence.

"Margaret?"

"Um?"

"I've wanted to talk to you for a long time . . ."

She sat up and looked at him. "Micah, we talk all the time."

"I know, but this is special, and I felt the need to let you—well, to let you find your way, first. But I think you have, so now, we need to talk."

Margaret searched to see Micah's expression, but it was too dark. His voice, however, held an urgency that could not be denied.

"What is it, Micah?"

"Well, like I said, I've wanted to talk about this for a long time." He paused.

"What is it? This is me, Margaret. You can say anything to me, Micah."

"I know . . . it's just . . . Oh, for heaven's sake! I'm worse than a love-struck teenager—I don't know any other way to say this, except, Margaret will you marry me?" He rushed on, "I know you love me, and I feel the same for you, and—well, will you?"

Margaret felt the rush of joy sweep through her. Micah loved her. Of course, he loved her, but even he realized it, and she loved him, but—.

Her joy faded.

"Micah, I do love you, but I've been sitting here thinking ever since we left that hospital, and I've made a decision I can't force you into."

"What decision, Margaret?"

She hesitated.

"You can tell me anything," he quoted.

She chuckled. "Yes, I can. I've decided I want to adopt Quinthia, if Andy agrees. He's going to die soon, and that baby needs someone who loves her to take care of her. I want that someone to be me, but I have to work through a lot of things first."

"What things that I couldn't be a part of?"

"My anger, for one thing. I'm not sure I believe Andy's story about what happened that night. He says it wasn't date rape, but why would Angela lie?"

"Maybe neither of them lied, Margaret. Have you ever heard two witnesses tell about a traffic accident. They tell conflicting stories, but when examined closely, they both told the truth from their perspective."

"Maybe," Margaret said, "but I have to work that all out, and I need to do it before I commit to caring for Quinthia. That child is really special, and I want to take care of her, but I want to be sure my resentment won't spill over into my treatment of her."

Micah squeezed Margaret's hand. "You may never lose all your resentment, but you'd never lash out at an innocent child. You may worry about it, but God and I know better."

Margaret forced a weak smile. "I'm glad you're so sure, because I really want to do this. She has so many needs, and I can at least provide the love."

She bit her lower lip, looked at Micah, and shook her head. "But I can't ask you to take on the financial responsibility for both of us."

Micah's only question was, "And how will you be able to provide her medical expenses?"

"Micah, I'm surprised at you. I don't know how, but God does, and He'll take care of it."

"You have grown, and I'm so pleased, but what makes you think I wouldn't like to have a black-haired, brown-eyed, teddy bear-loving little girl?"

"Are you serious?" Margaret asked, afraid to even hope. "We're not kids anymore, and she's sick, I mean, really sick. And if she does go into remission like they hope, she'll be loud and rambunctious, and she'll turn into a rebellious teenager, and we won't be able to send her home. She'll already be home."

"I know, and I'd love it. Cora and I never had children, and I've always felt I missed a lot. Isn't it wonderful God has given me this second chance? So will you marry me?"

"You do have a one-track mind, my good man," she said as she slipped into his arms and turned her face up to accept his kiss.

"And, yes, I'll marry you."

Margaret could hardly wait to hear how Andy felt about her and Micah's desire to adopt Quinthia.

"It is quite a surprise," Andy said. "I never dreamed anyone I knew would take Quinthia after all the family turned us down. They were all afraid of the leukemia. I wracked my brain so many days and nights trying to think of anyone who would be willing to take a sick child, let alone someone who was qualified to care for one. It's almost more than I can believe."

Margaret nodded. "I'm sure Micah mentioned the age factor."

Micah moved to her side and laid an arm around her waist.

"Yes. We talked about it, but you aren't as old as my parents were, and if they were alive, they would have been my first choice."

Margaret glanced at Micah and continued. "Our biggest concern is whether we can be taught to deal with Quinthia's medical problems."

"I don't know why you would have any more trouble learning than anyone else."

The room grew silent until Andy continued. "Have you two thought about the horrendous cost involved in caring for a child like Quinthia?"

Micah spoke first. "We've talked about it, and quite frankly, it terrifies us, but we believe God will provide whatever we need. Neither of us is extravagant, and we believe we can cope."

He paused, and Margaret asked, "Is there any insurance available at all?"

"I have a policy on her from my job, but now that the leukemia has been diagnosed, I don't know whether or not you could continue her coverage. If not, I'm sure a new policy would be out of the question."

Margaret searched Micah's face before she went any further. "I think we should check into that. I want Quinthia. Even in only these few encounters, I've grown to love her deeply, but we have to consider whether we really will be able to meet her needs. It wouldn't be a service to her to take her, and then not be able to provide the medical care she must have."

Andy looked up. "I've been talking to one of the social workers here at the hospital, and she's made an appointment for me to meet with a family services caseworker next week. She may be able to offer some input."

Margaret wanted to talk to the family services caseworker immediately. They needed to get started with whatever legalities were involved in adopting Quinthia. She and Micah could see Andy grow weaker each day. She knew the only thing keeping his strength up was his desire to see Quinthia's future assured. But Andy insisted they had to wait for his prearranged appointment.

Chapter Twenty-five

Kathy squealed and bounced up and down when Margaret told her the news. "Come over and sit down and tell me all about it."

When Margaret arrived at Kathy's home, she led Margaret to the kitchen table and set a cup of tea in front of her. Ed was at his job, but Kathy had been given the afternoon off while some computer updates were being done at her office. She'd asked Margaret to lunch with her and Desmond.

"Oh, Margaret," Kathy gushed, "I've been prayin' for this for so long. I just knew God would put you two together. You're perfect for one another—but, what took you so long?"

Margaret spluttered. "You've been praying for this?"

"Well, of course, girl! You two spend most of your time together anyway." She served the sandwiches and asked Margaret to offer a prayer of thanks. By that time, Desmond was in a full-blown fuss, so Kathy started to spoon strained peas and carrots into him at an amazing speed. The little boy was ravenous, and he seemed to barely take time to breath between bites.

"This will be perfect," Kathy exclaimed.

Margaret laughed. "Well, I'm so glad you approve!"

"So when's the wedding?" Kathy continued to poke the spoon at Desmond.

"In a few weeks."

"A few weeks? Why so long?"

"You sound just like Micah."

"I can imagine. What's the delay?"

"Kathy! I need a dress, and Micah can't perform his own ceremony. He has to clear a date with one of his preacher friends."

"Okay," Kathy said as she wiped a damp cloth over Desmond's squirming face. "So what kind of dress do you want? Something with a hoop and a long train?"

"I don't think so." Margaret laughed at Kathy's enthusiasm.

"What about bridesmaids?"

"Only a matron-of-honor. It'll be a small wedding—at least the wedding party will be. I don't know how to keep the wedding itself small when a 175-member congregation is invited, plus who-knows-how-many from congregations where Micah preached before."

"Wow! You do have some planning to do." Kathy bit into her sandwich. After several moments she asked, "So tell me, what do you have planned?"

"Well, for starters, I'm hoping my matron-of-honor will be a true friend and lady named Kathy Johnson. Will you?"

Kathy jumped to her feet and came to hug Margaret and squeal, "Yes. Oh, yes!" She suddenly straightened, worry creasing her brows. "What'll I wear?"

"Clothes, of course," Margaret teased.

"Margaret, I mean it. What'll I wear?"

"I'll make us both something."

Margaret decided to tell Kathy about Quinthia. "Kathy, Micah and I need your prayers, and I'd like to tell you about it."

Kathy leaned over and patted Margaret's hand. "You know we'll pray for you anytime. Now, what has you so intense all of a sudden?"

"Well," Margaret began, "it's a long story, but Micah and I want to adopt a little girl, and we need your prayers to help us accomplish that."

"What little girl? When did you decide that? Does Micah agree? How old is—"

"Whoa, Kathy! I can't answer all those questions as fast as you're asking. Just give me a few minutes, and I'll tell you all about it."

Kathy gave a contrite nod. "Okay, so shoot. And be quick. I'm dying of curiosity."

Margaret had never told anyone but Micah about Andy before, and the words came hard at first, but as she reached the end of their story, she told Kathy about the first time she saw Quinthia.

Her voice lilted, and she fairly gushed. "Kathy, she is absolutely beautiful. She has big, gorgeous eyes, and her hair will be dark when it grows back in. It already lays in tiny ringlets."

"A wedding and a little girl all at once!" Kathy exclaimed. "You do know how to start a new life!"

"The problem is, we don't know what legal steps we need to take. We have a lot of ground work to do before we can even get started, and Andy's running out of time."

"You do have your hands full. You're gonna need a lot of help."

"Probably, but I'll manage, with God's help, so you start praying double duty, you hear?"

"I hear, and you got it," Kathy said. "You got it, lady."

Margaret and Micah continued to visit Quinthia, and at Quinthia's insistence Margaret made a hat for Winston; then she started her wedding suit. She focused on each task before her with a relentless drive until whatever she tackled was finished.

Poor Cat finally gave up begging Margaret for extra attention and frequently turned to Micah for the strokes down her back or the extra portion of food.

Margaret rolled her eyes and laughed when she acknowledged to Micah, "I think I'm being displaced from her pedestal."

Kathy called and asked, "Have you set a date yet?"

"Not yet," Margaret hedged. She and Micah wanted to wait until Andy talked to the family services caseworker. The wedding would be tucked into whatever time fit between any legal or social work appointments they needed to meet in order to adopt Quinthia.

"Well, girl, you better get it together. You still have to order flowers and a cake, and somebody has to decorate the reception tables. You have loads to do."

"I know, Kathy, I know. I do have my suit done, except for the buttons, and I cut out yours this afternoon. If I can get to the machine tomorrow, you should be able to try it on the next day. Will you have time to come by on your way home from work and let me mark the hem?"

"I'll make time. Is there anything I can do in the meantime to help?"

"I don't know, Kathy. Why?"

"Well, I've been thinking. If you don't mind, I'd like to make the centerpieces for the reception tables."

"Kathy, that would be wonderful, but only if you let me pay you for the supplies and your time."

"Supplies, yes. Time, no way."

"Kathy—"

"Don't you 'Kathy' me. You've done all kinds of things for me. This will be the Johnson family's wedding gift to you and Micah."

"Are you sure you'll have time? You do have that new job, and Ed and Desmond to tend."

"I have more time than you do. Tell me what color you want, and leave me be. I'll knock your socks off."

Margaret laughed. "Deal! By the time I get to the wedding day, I'm sure I'll be ready to try to relax. Oh, Kathy?"

"Yes?"

"Don't get too elaborate with your plans. We don't want to spend a lot on the wedding. We're going to need every penny we can scrape together to take care of Quinthia, if we get her."

"Let me think about it, and I'll get back with you. What have you found out about Quinthia?"

"Nothing, yet. I won't know anything until Andy meets with the social worker on Friday."

"Oh good! That's the same day I'm supposed to come by. You should know something by the time I get there to try on my suit."

"I certainly hope so," Margaret said. "I keep wondering if the authorities will think we're too old or too poor to cope with Quinthia. I ask myself those questions, so we have to expect the courts to ask."

"Margaret?"

"What?"

"Shut up! You know you and Micah are perfect for that child, and God knows that, too. If you must talk about it, talk to him. He'll listen, and he's the one who's able to do whatever it takes to fix it up."

Margaret laughed out loud. "Yes, ma'am. You're right—again. I'll do just that, and I'll see you day after tomorrow."

Margaret hung up the phone and went back to her sewing room.

As she stitched the elaborate buttons on the creamy soft-blue wool, she did pray, long and hard. She finished with the buttons and hung the suit. Micah would be by soon to take her back to the hospital. It was her turn to spend the night again.

Chapter Twenty-six

$\mathcal{M}$icah came for Margaret at eleven o'clock on Friday morning. They were to meet Andy at the hospital. His appointment with the social worker had been set for eight o'clock, and he was to report his findings to them over lunch.

Margaret was ready at the door when Micah arrived, but he took her hand and drew her back inside.

"Let's sit down a minute, honey," he said.

"Micah, I can't wait much longer to find out what Andy learned."

"We can both wait long enough to pray," Micah said gently.

Margaret was immediately contrite. "Of course we can."

They sat on the sofa together, and Micah held her hands.

They both bowed their heads in silent prayer for a few moments, then Micah spoke.

> "Father, our hearts are heavy right now, because our concern is for Quinthia. You know how we love her, and you know her daddy's condition. Father, if it's your will, help us to clear whatever hurdles we may face, and help us become Quinthia's new parents. Help us touch Andy, and show him your love, and guide him to your family. Help us comfort him and bless us all. Give us the strength to fulfill whatever you have in mind for us. We ask through Jesus for all these things. Amen."

When he finished, Micah led Margaret to the car. The drive had never seemed so long. Margaret's throat was dry, and her stomach gurgled violently—not the hungry rumbling she was used to—but a nervous volcanic gurgle.

What if they were too old to adopt a child? What if their income was too small? What if there were some unknown restrictions they couldn't surmount?

"Can't you go any faster?" she asked Micah when he stopped at a traffic light.

"Not unless you want me to get a ticket." He laid his free hand over hers. "He'll still be there, and the news won't change in the few extra minutes it takes us to get there."

"I know, but I'm dying of anxiety."

"If it's any comfort, so am I, but we'll know something soon. There's the hospital in the next block."

They stood silent in the elevators and they walked briskly down the hall to Quinthia's room.

Quinthia squealed. "Marge! Micah! Did you bring my pigs back?"

Margaret smiled at the pet name Quinthia had given her. "Right here, sweetie."

A nurse entered the room with a wheelchair. "Ready, Miss Quinthia? Play time."

"Yeah! Let's go! I wanna play with the piano."

"We'll see," the nurse said. She turned to Andy. "We'll be back in a couple of hours."

"I'll be in the cafeteria, or back here, if you need me," Andy said.

The nurse nodded and wheeled Quinthia to the elevators.

Andy turned to Micah and Margaret. "Shall we go?"

"I thought you'd never ask," Margaret said.

As soon as they had their food and found a table, Margaret asked, "So what did you find out, Andy. I can't stand this suspense."

"Well, it wasn't as informative as I had hoped, but I did learn privately arranged adoptions are frowned on by the state—"

Margaret blurted, "Does that mean we don't have a chance?"

"It makes it harder, but in cases like Quinthia's, they're more lenient."

"So we can do it?" Micah asked.

"I don't know. It all depends on a lot of different factors."

"Like?" Margaret asked.

"You'll have to file an application to adopt with the Division of Family Services. They'll do a background check and take a financial statement. I understand they ask for references, and they'd like one to be from your local clergyman. You may have a tough time getting one of those," he teased.

"None of that sounds too difficult," Micah said. "Did she give any indication of what the financial requirements would be?"

"Not in specific numbers. She did say they'd be more interested in the emotional care than lots of monetary pluses. On the other hand, she said they'll want to be sure the adoptive parents could provide for her physical needs, and that does include her medical expenses."

"Oh, Micah, can we do that?"

"Day to day expenses, yes, but as for her medical expenses, in view of what I've seen here in the past several days, I don't see how."

"What about her health insurance?" Margaret asked. "Can't we just continue the policy she has?"

"I'm afraid not," Andy said. "I checked. It's a COBRA policy I extended from my former job. Government policy only requires them to carry us a certain period of time, and it's almost up. To be honest, at the time I took the policy, I didn't expect either of us to live long enough to reach the end of the contract. Since we have, the company will use any means they can to dump her."

"I'm sure you're right," Micah said.

"Well, we have to do something," Margaret said.

"The caseworker did say that in her opinion a married couple would get preference over a single parent placement, just because of the demands made by the illness . . . So . . . the first thing you need to do is get married."

"I can do that!" said Micah.

Margaret frowned. "Micah, I'm serious. We have to *do* something."

"We will, honey. We'll pray, and we'll get married, and we'll go fill out the application. They can't tell us yes or no until we do all that. And we'll trust God to take care of it."

"Micah!"

"Margaret! What else can we do?"

She bowed her head in submission. "You're right. I know you are, but this trust stuff is so hard sometimes."

"Nobody said it would be easy."

"When can we go see the caseworker?" Margaret asked Andy.

"Any time, I guess. You should probably call for an appointment, but she seemed willing to talk to you."

"Do you have her number?"

"Right here."

"Micah, let's go call."

"We will, my dear, but could I finish my lunch first?"

She forced herself into a calmer state of mind and replied, "If you must." When she burst out laughing, she saw Micah and Andy had joined her.

Micah made the call and set an appointment for Monday morning. Margaret didn't think she could wait, but she knew she must.

Kathy came by that evening to have her hem measured, as they had arranged. She stepped in the door and said, "So?"

"So we don't know anything yet. We have an appointment Monday to make an application to adopt, and we're praying."

"So it's all under control, or it will be when I make a few calls."

"What calls?"

"To the church deacons' and elders' wives. We'll call the whole congregation and get everyone else praying. It's all under control, like I said."

A sense of humility overwhelmed Margaret. "It is, isn't it?"

"Yeah, it is."

On Monday, Micah and Margaret went to the Division of Family Services office to meet with a Miss Tucker. They filled out the application and turned in a financial statement and references.

"We'll run the references, and we want to have separate interviews with each of you in a couple of weeks," Miss Tucker said.

"A couple of weeks!" Margaret exclaimed. "We're running out of time. Quinthia's father is dying."

"Mrs. Ceradsky, I know we're racing the clock, and believe me, I'm on your side. But there are certain procedures that have to take place to meet the requirements of the law. You've told me you're planning your wedding. Why don't you go ahead with that, and just sort of forget this is in the works. By the time the wedding is over, I should have some answers for you."

"But—"

"Mrs. Ceradsky, I'm really sorry, but I can only rush this so much. I'll do my best, but it'll take at least two weeks—maybe more."

"I understand," Margaret said. "And I'm sorry. It's just that Quinthia is going to need someone soon, and waiting is killing me."

"I'm really sorry."

"I think we need to go, Margaret, and let Miss Tucker get started on this."

"Yes, of course. Again, I'm sorry I'm so impatient."

"At least I don't doubt the strength of your desire," Miss Tucker said and chuckled.

Margaret and Micah decided the Saturday two weeks away would be as soon as they could be ready for the wedding.

Micah said, "We don't need to send too many invitations. I have one living brother—"

"And I have one sister," Margaret said.

"One to the whole congregation which will be read from the pulpit and printed in the bulletin—"

"And a few friends from out of town."

"The congregation in Texas, where I preached, and the one in Arkansas, the two in Kansas, and the one in Iowa."

Margaret grabbed her head. "Will the building hold them all?"

"No, but they won't all come. But they will want to be invited just the same."

"How do I plan cake and punch?"

"Just do gobs, and what isn't used that day can be frozen to use at fellowships later."

"Whatever you say. I can see life as a minister's wife is going to be interesting."

"Guess so."

Micah drove her to the florist's shop. They looked at pictures, and

Margaret chose a small nosegay of roses and baby's breath, just as she had envisioned.

When the florist quoted a price, Margaret gasped. "Oh, no, I don't think so. You see, this is a second marriage for both of us, and we're adopting a very ill little girl. Can you suggest something less expensive?"

The lady thought a moment. "Well, gladoli can be worked up very pretty and quite economically."

"I can't quite envision it," Margaret said.

"Wait," the clerk said. She went to the design table and fashioned a light blue bow of wide ribbon with long streamers.

Then she went to the cooler and brought out three full-blooming stems of white gladoli. She clustered them with the bow and cradled them in her arms.

"It's called an arm bouquet, and it costs less than half the price of the nosegay, and gives you a large splash of bloom."

Margaret turned to Micah. "What do you think? I like it."

"It's pretty, and if you like it, I love it."

"Do you really, or is that the diplomat speaking?"

"Both," Micah admitted. "I'm really rather indifferent. I'll be happy with whatever you chose."

The clerk spoke. "We can break the buds out and make boutonnieres for the men. They really are attractive."

Margaret pulled a couple of fabric scraps out. "Could you match the ribbons to these colors in the two bouquets?"

"I'm sure we can, but for pictures, I suggest a deeper color to emphasize the contrast."

"Pictures!" Margaret gasped. "I forgot. Who can do pictures?"

"I can recommend an excellent photographer," the clerk said.

"No, I don't think we can afford a professional," Margaret said.

The clerk shrugged, and went to get some ribbon samples.

While she was gone, Micah said, "Bruce could probably do a good job with photos."

"Good idea. I've seen some of his snapshots. Let's ask him."

They placed their order, and Micah said, "Wait here, and I'll give her my credit card for the deposit."

"But flowers are my responsibility," Margaret told him.

"So pay me back later. I get a percentage back when I use my card."

Margaret didn't argue the point, but it seemed to take an inordinate amount of time for Micah to process the charge.

Finally, he came back. "Now where?"

"I don't really know. We need a cake, but I have no idea where to go, or for how many people."

"Don't the grocery store bakeries do wedding cakes?"

"I guess so."

"Let's go."

In the car, Micah said, "Why don't we get a medium-sized cake and ask some of the women to bake sheet cakes that could be frozen, if they're not all needed?"

"That sounds fine to me, if you're sure nobody would be offended."

"Why should they be? Some of our women are much better cooks than any grocery store bakery."

A half hour later, they ordered a three-tier wedding cake, gathered up nuts, mints, innumerable cans of juices, and bottles of ginger ale to make punch.

"Your trunk overfloweth," Margaret teased.

"I'm a little worried about how we're supposed to transport that cake when they get it done," Micah said.

"We'll ask Kathy to pick it up in her van."

"Good idea. Now, what else?"

"Napkins, plates, and cups. Are there forks at the church?"

"Some, but disposable stuff would be better."

"Onward, to Paper Warehouse." Margaret enjoyed this. At last they were making progress.

"Don't you think we should wait until you and Kathy decide how many tablecloths you need?"

"To quote one of my favorite persons," Margaret said, "'Good idea.'"

She leaned against Micah and glowed in the comfort of how well they fit together.

Micah gazed down. "There is one more really important thing."

"I can't imagine what. The car's full."

"This is a rather small item," Micah said. "Come on."

He drove her to the mall.

"Micah?"

"Sh-h-h. Come along, my dear."

He led her to the front of a large jewelry store.

"Oh, no, Micah. We can't afford rings. We'll need our money for Quinthia."

"I know, and I have a suggestion. I just want to see if it'll work. Do you have your old wedding rings?"

"Yes, you know I wear them on my right hand."

"I still have Cora's rings, too. How do you feel about having both rings broken down, and the stones reset in a new band for you? Sort of a blending of both our complete lives. I don't expect to forget Cora, and I don't think you'll forget Henry—but I do expect our love to benefit by our relationships with them. What do you think?"

"I think it's a lovely idea, Micah. Let's go see if they can do it."

Doing it was not the problem. Having it ready in two weeks was the real issue, but the jeweler promised to put in a rush order, and he was sure it would be honored.

Micah's phone rang, and he stepped outside the store to talk while Margaret finalized a time to pick up the rings.

"Well," Micah said once they were back in the car, "that should just about top off what we can do for the wedding today."

"Wrong," Margaret said emphatically.

"Now what? I'm getting tired."

"So am I. I'm exhausted, but I don't think even a preacher can get married in this state without a license."

"A license! If we must!"

Micah laughed and Margaret's heart skipped a beat when she saw those cute little crinkles around his eyes, and the quirk at the corner of his mouth.

"It's a good thing I love you, Margaret Ceradsky, because I would not venture off to the county clerk's office today for any other reason. I have another appointment soon, but I think we have time for this."

"And it's a good thing I love you, or I'd be looking for a livelier model."

"Oh, no, you wouldn't," he volleyed. "I saw you slip those shoes off and slide them under the seat."

"Rats. Caught again."

Micah glanced across at her. "We have one more stop to make."

Margaret groaned. "I don't think I have the energy, Micah. Is it really important?"

"I think so," he said as he wheeled into the church parking lot.

Margaret noticed there were several cars already parked there, and still others followed them in and parked alongside them.

"What's going on, Micah?"

He turned off the engine, turned to her, and took both her hands. "You are about to witness the fruits of your labor, my dear."

Margaret studied his smile, and the brightness of his eyes. "What labor?"

"Your labor with Andy and with Quinthia. That call back at the jewelry store was Andy. He wants to be baptized. He'll be here any minute."

"Oh, Micah," she gasped, before she fumbled in her purse for a tissue. "I am so glad. We've prayed long and hard for this. I was so afraid he would wait too long."

"I know," Micah agreed. "Now if we can just get the adoption finalized in time."

Chapter Twenty~seven

Saturday morning dawned sunny and beautiful. Margaret rushed through toast and jam and a cup of hot chocolate. She stroked Cat and fed her; then she dashed upstairs to dress in slacks and a frilly blouse. Kathy would arrive soon to take her to the church to do one last check.

Margaret had just finished running the brush through her hair when the doorbell rang. She grabbed her purse on the way to the door.

"Ready, girl?" Kathy asked, after she greeted Margaret.

"I think so."

Kathy drove and chattered all the way to the building. "Just wait 'til you see what I have planned. I'm gonna set things up while you're checkin' out everything else."

"What in the world are you going to do with all those balloons? The whole back of the van is full."

"You'll see."

LaMont and his friends met them at the door. "We've come to help."

"Great," Kathy said. "We can use some muscle."

Margaret went to see if the flowers had arrived while LaMont, Hector, and Yin Ling helped Kathy carry in the decorations she had prepared.

Margaret stepped inside the auditorium and smiled at the two large baskets of white gladioli on the dais. The effect was beautiful.

Margaret sank onto a back pew and just gazed for several moments. How blessed she was to have Micah, and soon Quinthia. It amazed her how much her life had changed in the past few months.

She couldn't have stopped her prayers of thanks even if she'd tried, for she realized full well that God's grace had wrought her new happiness.

After an undefined time of reflection, Margaret went to find the rest of the flowers. She didn't want to discover anything missing at the last moment.

The huge boxes sat in one of the classrooms. Each item was labeled, and she ticked off boutonnieres for all the men, and corsages for the servers at the reception, but there were no bouquets for herself, or for Kathy.

She replaced the lid and saw a note taped to it. "Bride's flowers in the nursery."

Then she remembered Kathy had told her most brides used that room to dress because it was private, and there was an adjoining bathroom and a full-length mirror.

Margaret climbed the stairs to inspect the bouquets. She stared at two squarish boxes, much too short for arm bouquets. She frowned and glanced at her watch. It was getting late to make any adjustments.

She slipped the lid off one box. Inside a nest of tissue sat one of the most beautiful nosegays Margaret had ever seen. It was made of little pink roses, a puffy little flower she thought might be bachelor buttons—some light blue, and some dark, and lots of baby's breath.

She bit her lower lip. It was beautiful, and exactly what she'd picked at first, but surely the florist should have understood the change in her order.

She went to the other box. It was clearly marked "Bride" on the lid.

Margaret looked inside and gasped. There, on its bed of tissue, sat a larger nosegay of ivory roses with the slightest blush of pink in the center. Baby's breath peeked out among the beautiful creamy blooms. Pale blue streamers cascaded down from the handle. A card rested on edge, and Margaret opened it.

My dear Margaret,

I've written this note because Kathy has sternly forbidden me to see you before the ceremony today. Please don't be upset, but I watched you at the flower shop, and I knew how much you liked the round bouquets, so I secretly had the florist change our order. I wanted this day to be as perfect for you as I know it will be for me. I'll love you always.

Micah

Margaret felt the tears sting her eyes, and she rushed to the bathroom to collect a tissue. *Stop that,* she told herself. *Brides aren't supposed to cry on their wedding day, even if they are tears of joy.*

She gently replaced the box lid and decided to go see how Kathy was fairing. She descended the basement stairs and rounded the corner to the fellowship hall.

"Oh, my," Margaret said when she saw the room. "Kathy, just look at what you've done."

"Do you like it?"

"How could I not love it? Look at those beautiful flowers. What are they? Carnations?"

"Sort of."

"What do you mean, sort of?"

Kathy grinned. "Well, they do look like carnations, but actually, they're tissues."

"No!" Margaret stepped closer to one of the tables. Each one had a white tablecloth with three wide bands of blue ribbon running down the center of it. Scattered in symmetrical spaces lay clusters of three carnations with greenery.

"They're beautiful," Margaret said, "but how did you have time?"

Kathy laughed. "All I did was go buy the ribbon and a couple of boxes of tissue. Ed's been the one tearing and folding and wiring. I don't think he wants to see one more tissue for a while."

Margaret laughed. "I don't suppose so." She glanced up and saw two huge interlinking hearts on the wall, fully outlined in the paper flowers.

"Poor Ed. His fingers must be sore."

"Naw. Truth be known, it gave him something to do after work.

He's still burned out on television. LaMont and his friends are the ones who were stretched to the limit blowing up all these balloons, and helpin' to hang 'em, too."

Margaret looked overhead at the blue and white balloons all over the ceiling. Between clusters, Kathy had placed some honeycombed bells in blue.

Margaret reached over and hugged Kathy. "I've never seen this old cement-block room look so pretty. You've done a great job, Kathy."

"You're welcome, but you helped me first, and we're not done yet. Let's get goin'. Time's flyin'."

Margaret never was quite sure how Kathy managed it, but by four that afternoon Margaret and Micah stood in the reception line and accepted congratulations from what seemed like a hundred legions of well-wishers.

Toward the end of the line, Margaret looked up, then laid her hand on Micah's arm. When his gaze met hers, she nodded toward someone a few feet away.

They both squatted and held arms out to receive the little girl who ran toward them.

"Marge, you're pretty," Quinthia said before she began to squirm. "You're squishin' me, Micah."

He laughed and loosened his hold, then lifted Quinthia in his arms and stood to greet her father.

"Hello, Andy. We're so glad both of you felt well enough to join us today. It means a lot to us to have you here."

"Yes, it does," Margaret agreed.

Andy gave a rueful grin. "Weddings aren't exactly my thing, but Quinthia wouldn't hear of missing this one!"

"Of course not," Margaret said. Her heart swelled with pride when she looked at Micah holding his arm full of pink cotton-candy ruffles, and a wide-brimmed organza hat.

Andy turned to Micah and asked, "Mind if I borrow Margaret for a few moments?"

Micah raised his brows in mock consternation. "Only for a few, Andy. She's all mine now!"

Andy chuckled and said, "I promise, I'll only keep her long enough for a few very vital words."

Margaret allowed him to lead her to the back of the room where he turned and said, "Margaret, I have a lot to learn about God and how he works, but I have learned enough to know I owe you an apology for what happened between myself and Angela, and I need your forgiveness for her death. I don't know if you can give me that, or not, but I want you to know I am truly sorry."

Margaret felt the tears well, and she swallowed down the all-familiar bile that surfaced every time she thought of Angela. It took her a long moment to compose herself enough to speak.

"Andy, there was a time when I would not have been able to even consider forgiving you. I wanted to punish you beyond anything you could begin to imagine." She hesitated and struggled for composure. "But I, too, have learned a good bit about God and his ways. I think we need to forgive one another—me for your sins, and you for mine."

Andy wrapped his frail arms around Margaret and hugged her, and Margaret felt a peace wash over her. She had already dismissed her wrath toward Andy, but his seeking forgiveness was the ultimate release for her. She could finally be at peace with all that had happened, and she could love Andy in the deepest sense of the word. When she returned Andy's hug, there was no longer any sense of bitterness or anger. She wanted only the best for Andy, and for his daughter. God was so good, even in horrible situations like the one they had just lived through. If he could change her so completely through this, she knew he would help her through whatever the future held.

She rested in Andy's embrace for a moment, then pulled back. "Come on, guy. We have party guests to attend to. "

Andy smiled and gave a mock bow. "Okay, Princess, I'll take you back to your Prince Charming."

They walked to Micah's side, where Quinthia reached for Margaret's hand. "Can I have some cake now?"

Margaret laughed before she handed the child over to Andy. "I think so, sweety. Have your daddy get you a piece, okay?"

The only thing to dampen this day was the knowledge that Quinthia's daddy had a very limited time left to enjoy his daughter.

The adoption was now legally finalized and Margaret and Micah had agreed to allow Andy to retain custody of Quinthia as long as he was able. Andy, however, felt she would adapt better if she moved into their home before he left this earth.

"I'll visit her every day, if you'll let me—"

"Certainly, we'll let you," Micah butted in.

Andy had insisted, "But she needs to get used to you before some sudden incident just dumps her into your lap."

"I agree," Margaret had said.

The three of them had discussed it, and they decided the weekend after the wedding would be a good time to move Quinthia into her new home.

In spite of Margaret's protests that they could honeymoon at home, Micah insisted they take a short trip to the Lake of the Ozarks.

"The phones don't work down there," he teased.

Margaret finally agreed, for although she knew the phones did work, nobody would dare call there unless it was a dire emergency!

Epilogue

On November 16, Margaret and Quinthia stood at the cemetery where Micah delivered Andrew Bartimus' eulogy, preached a plea for reconciliation to God to those present, and prayed one final prayer for Andy.

> "Father, please accept this your child into your bosom, and bless him until we come to meet him at your side. Be with us left here, and help us to care for Quinthia as he would want. Help us to guide her into the truth her daddy embraced so that she, too, may be reunited with him."

Margaret looked down at her daughter and smiled at the short black ringlets that framed her cherubic face. Her thin little arms and legs extended from her pink, ruffled dress like toothpicks stuck in a tin can, but Margaret knew she gained a few ounces every day. Soon she would be filled out and healthy.

Church members filed by and murmured words of condolence, and Margaret took great comfort in their expressions of sympathy. At last, Kathy and Ed came. Desmond sat on his daddy's lap while Kathy pushed.

Quinthia pulled on Margaret's hand. "Mommy Marge, can Desmond come over? Can he, please?"

"Of course, dear. The whole congregation has brought food, and you and Desmond can go into the recreation room and play all you want."

Kathy smiled. "That sounds good."

"What?"

"Mommy Marge," Kathy said.

"It sounds just great to me, too," Micah said, "but not as good as Daddy Micah."

He leaned over and kissed Margaret.

Kathy laughed. "You two act like newlyweds."

"We are," Micah declared. "Six weeks still qualifies."

He grew sober. "Today is the end of a sad time, but thanks to Mommy Marge, it's also the beginning of a more glorious time."

Kathy laughed. "Now that Quinthia's leukemia seems to be in remission, you ain't seen nothin' yet. Just wait 'til she really gets her strength back."

Micah gave an impish grin and winked at Margaret. "I think Andy would approve and say, 'Let the adventure begin.'"

Dear Reader,

I hope you enjoyed the journey Margaret and her friends made toward the Lord. It is my observation that although most of us do not confront a hurt so heinous as Margaret's or Micah's, we do often harbor those same feelings of outrage and a desire to strike back.

My prayer is that this book will help some of my readers with those struggles. For those who do not harbor such feelings, I hope you found the book to be an insight to hatred and bitterness and that you will be less reluctant to reach out to those suffering from the consequences.

I love to hear from my readers. Write to me or email me! Visit my web site often for updates on my latest works, my schedule for booksignings and lectures, and for lots of Christian links to help you in your daily walk with God. May we all follow in his steps and plan to meet in his presence some day.

In Christ,
Wilburta Arrowood

P.O. Box 869
Liberty, MO 61069-0869
wa@wilburtaarrowood.com
http://www.wilburtaarrowood.com

Other Books from Publishing Designs, Inc.

Authors: Gloria Ingram, Jane McWhorter, Foye Watkins, Sheila Butt, Cindy Colley
ISBN: 092954028X
Our Price: $8.95
Description: A doctrinal study of fundamentals revealing God's wishes over man's wishes. Since women greatly influence public worship, this book is a timely reminder of God's guidelines. Songs, harps, tithes, communion, kneeling, passover, prayer guide. Five topics: music, teaching, Lord's supper, prayer, and giving. Each topic examined from both the Old Testament and New Testament. Questions. Edited by James Andrews.

Author: Bobby Duncan
ISBN: 0929540255
Our Price: $7.95
Description: Easy to teach and study, yet challenging. First in a series of Inspiring Profiles. Thirteen lessons about Bible women from Eve to Lydia in outline form. Wicked Jezebel, courageous Esther, and more. Chapter questions.

Author: Teresa Hampton
ISBN: 0929540247
Our Price: $7.95
Description: Refreshing ideas and simple guidelines show women divine parameters for leadership. A how-to book for ladies who want to put away complaining, worrying, and gossiping, and step into God's service. Thirteen chapters with questions.

Author: Sheila Butt
ISBN: 0929540220
Our Price: $7.95
Description: How does a mother guide her children to love and serve God at every age? Sheila knows! Her work is biblically based and contains many examples

of mother-child relationships. Great for personal and group study; great for gifts. Chapter questions.

Author: Sheila Butt
ISBN: 0929540263
Our Price: $7.95
Description: A book of courage and power for women who are not satisfied with the world's standard of spirituality. Examine God's plan for your spiritual makeover.

Authors: Jane McWhorter, LeeAnn Duke, Debbie Kea, Bonnie Ruiz, Irene Taylor, Cindy Colley
ISBN: 0929540239
Our Price: $8.95
Description: Personal trials and responsibilities of Christian women. Deals with intimacy in marriage, motherhood, and being the wife of a church leader or missionary. Tackles controversial and unpopular issues pertaining to the role of women and immorality. Balanced and well written. For personal or class studies. Edited by Kerry Duke.

Author: Don and Jane McWhorter
ISBN: 092954000X
Our Price: $7.95
Description: Married or happy? Why not both? Reap benefits from Don and Jane's lasting marriage. Secrets of communication, commitment, and leadership. Solutions for "I do" vs. "I don't." Scripture-filled. Practical chapter questions.

Author: Don McWhorter
ISBN: 0929540123
Our Price: $7.95
Description: Are women in the church being swallowed up by worldly culture? Has the Feminist Movement received acceptance in the brotherhood? Should wives submit to their husbands? Join in a Bible study of the gender role controversy analyzing equality, divine hierarchy, silence. Also, hats, veils, hair cuts, clothes, and jewelry. Chapter summaries and questions.

Author: Cindy Colley
ISBN: 0929540042
Our Price: $6.95
Description: Divine accounts of the successes and failures of women. Portrays a variety of types of women. Today's Christian woman will be challenged to view her influence and to weave the moral fiber of future generations. Thirteen lessons. Chapter questions.

Author: Jo Ann Mills
ISBN: 0929540131
Our Price: $6.95
Description: A grandmother writes a book about life. Chapter titles are taken from quilt patterns: "The Cross," "Double Wedding Rings," etc. Each of the thirteen lessons is laid out in three sections: The Devotion, The Application, Notes for Teacher or Presenter. Chapter questions.

Author: Anita Whitaker
ISBN: 0929540328
Our Price: $8.95
Description: Compromising one's morality, character, influence, tolerance of sin, and commitment. These are a few of many dangerous darts hurled at young women. This book exposes addiction lures, dating traps, gossip pools, and other dangers in a concise manner. Chapter questions.

Author: Janie Craun
ISBN: 0929540336
Our Price: $8.95
Description: Ancient questions—today's answers: Am I my brother's keeper? Is anything too hard for the Lord? Why are ye so fearful? Foreword by Wayne Jackson. Thirteen lessons. Questions throughout the text.

To order books:
Toll free: 888-662-1006
Fax: 256-533-4302
www.publishingdesigns.com

PD
Books with Class
PUBLISHING DESIGNS, INC.
P.O. Box 3241 • Huntsville, Alabama 35810
256-533-4301 • jbapdi@juno.com